WINTER
TIDINGS

PRAIRIE RIVER

WINTER TIDINGS

KRISTIANA GREGORY

SCHOLASTIC INC.
New York Toronto London Auckland Sydney
Mexico City New Delhi Hong Kong Buenos Aires

No part of this publication may be reproduced in whole or in part, or stored in a retrieval system, or transmitted in any form or by any means, electronic, mechanical, photocopying, recording, or otherwise, without written permission of the publisher. For information regarding permission, write to Scholastic Inc., Attention: Permissions Department, 557 Broadway, New York, NY 10012.

ISBN 0-439-44001-7

Copyright © 2004 by KK Publishing Corp. All rights reserved. Published by Scholastic Inc., 557 Broadway, New York, NY 10012. SCHOLASTIC and associated logos are trademarks and/or registered trademarks of Scholastic Inc.

12 11 10 9 8 7 6 5 4 3 2 1   3 4 5 6 7 8/0
                                                              40

Printed in the U.S.A.
First printing, October 2004

Table of Contents

PRAIRIE RIVER

WINTER TIDINGS

CHAPTER ONE

⸺◆⸺

December 1865

Gray winter skies darkened the Kansas prairie. Wind swirled Nessa's skirt around her ankles and blew the fringe of her shawl as she led Wildwing from the corral. She struggled with the heavy log gate, latching it behind her. The colt was still too young to ride, but she wanted to walk him to the creek for a fresh drink of water. Although there was ice along the riverbank, it would be thin enough to break with a rock.

Through the wind she could hear the faint sound of a trumpet. She looked toward the fort to see a soldier lifting what appeared to be a spyglass to his eye. He was watching the Santa Fe Trail. In the distance, a rider was approaching Fort Larned at a gallop. The air was speckled with whirling snow.

Nessa could see the horseman disappear behind a knoll, then a moment later rise as if on a wave at sea. Her heart quickened. She hoped there wasn't trouble with the Indians. Even though peace treaties had been signed, some townsfolk had been whispering rumors about rene-

1

gade warriors ready to fight. The murder and scalping of two ranchers was still fresh in everyone's mind.

It was late afternoon and dark clouds in the north hinted of a coming storm. The wind felt cold through Nessa's dress. She let Wildwing drink, then hurried home along the creek trail so she would be back in time to help Mrs. Lockett prepare supper. As the wind pulled at her skirt, she ducked her head to avoid the stinging flakes. Mrs. Lockett's boardinghouse was up ahead, a snug stone building with smoke curling up from its chimney. Nessa had lived here for eight months, since running away from the orphanage in Missouri.

Home, she thought. She glanced at the upstairs window where she had a tiny room to herself. She couldn't wait until tonight, when she could crawl under her warm buffalo robe and listen to the storm.

In the kitchen Nessa tied on her long white apron, then began setting the table for six. Bowls, spoons, teacups, and plates of fresh bread. Two guests would be joining them for supper this evening. As she slid a pan of pudding into the black iron stove, Rolly burst in from the front porch.

"Nessa, guess what?" he said, out of breath. He was fifteen with blue eyes and wild blond hair. His knees showed through holes in his dungarees and a slingshot was tucked under a suspender.

Still at the stove, Nessa smiled without looking up at him. She didn't want to burn her hand. "You caught a rabbit?"

"Better," he said. "Ten times better."

The voice of a young girl called from the parlor. Minnie was Rolly's six-year-old sister. She appeared in the doorway holding a pencil and her diary. The opened pages revealed she had been drawing a horse. "Did you see an Indian?" she asked. Minnie had the same blue eyes as her brother and her blond pigtails were unraveled at the ends.

"Nope," he said, "just a trader. He came into the sutler's store while I was buying Ma's butter. Said there's a white girl livin' with the Cheyenne not far from here. She was captured by a war party that killed her whole family."

Nessa wiped her hands on her apron. She sat down, concern on her face. "Everyone was killed?" She tried to imagine what this girl must feel, to lose everyone at once and so violently. Nessa knew what it was like to be without family, but the memory of her parents was dim. "How old is she?" she asked.

"About your age," Rolly said. "Fourteen or so. The trader said she was wearing a buckskin dress and moccasins, that the only reason he knew she wasn't an Indian was on account of her green eyes. The girl whispered a few words of English to him, but a squaw dragged her away before he could talk to her."

A rush of cold air filled the kitchen as Mrs. Lockett came in through the back door. She pushed it closed with her hip and set her basket of eggs on the table. She was plump with red cheeks, and her upswept hair was held in place by small combs. Before she had a chance to hang her shawl on the peg, Minnie had reported the news, plus some extra she made up.

". . . and she needs a bath, Mama, real bad, and also a new place to live. She's an orphan, like Nessa. Can we keep her?"

Mrs. Lockett held her red hands over the stove to warm them. "My word, Minnie," she said, "of course, she's welcome with us. But this poor girl ain't a little pet that you keep in a box. I reckon she's had her share of heartache, and it'll be quite an ordeal rescuin' her. It might take weeks. Misunderstandin's with the Indians could cause more trouble, so we all have to be patient, can't rush a thing like this. Son, is the army gonna try to get her?"

"I ain't sure," he said. "Folks in the store were saying that the colonel wants to trade her for some horses, then bring her to the fort by Christmas."

During this conversation Rolly had been leaning against a pantry shelf, his hands behind his back. A freshly frosted chocolate cake was inches away from his fingers. When his mother looked away and began beating eggs into a bowl, he quickly brought a clump of icing to his lips.

Minnie and Nessa exchanged glances, then looked at Mrs. Lockett. The woman was measuring cups of flour. "Son, I'm ready for that butter now," she said.

Rolly's jaw dropped open. "Oh, Ma, I'm sorry, I got to talking with the folks and plumb forgot. Be right back."

The door slammed with a *whoosh* of cold air as he darted outside. It would be nearly an hour before he returned. Mrs. Lockett reached into a drawer of the sideboard and pulled out a flat knife. She handed it to Nessa.

"My dear," she said with a weary smile, "would you be so kind as to repair the hole Rolly made in our cake?"

CHAPTER TWO

———⊰◆⊱———

A Stranger in the Night

Storm clouds hid the setting sun. Nessa watched the sky from the kitchen window while she and Minnie dried the supper dishes. After putting away the cups and saucers, they sat in the parlor with the two gentlemen guests. An older man was playing dominoes with Rolly, the other was reading a newspaper by the light of the fire.

Minnie squeezed herself beside Nessa into the wing-back chair and, with her journal in her lap, resumed drawing her horse, but now with someone riding it.

"Who's that?" Nessa asked, indicating the stick figure wearing a dress.

"That orphaned girl who's living with Indians," she answered. "I want her to have a pony so she won't be too lonesome."

"That's very kind of you, Minnie." Nessa kissed the top of her head, then gazed at the fire. She remembered what it felt like to be alone in the world, with no family, surrounded by strangers. It seemed such a long time ago, even though Nessa had only been living with the Locketts for nearly a year.

Lord Jesus, she prayed, *please watch over this girl and bring her people who will truly care for her.*

Mrs. Lockett came into the room and sat at her roll-top desk where she took out a sheet of stationery and a quill pen. She dipped the quill into the ink jug, then, in beautiful penmanship, gracefully moved her hand across the page as if she were painting a picture. Nessa was close enough to see the words, *my darling,* and knew Mrs. Lockett was writing to her husband again. Though the Civil War had ended eight months earlier, Captain Lockett was still in a hospital back East recovering from wounds. He had sent word that he would return as soon as possible.

The clock on the mantel chimed eight. Mrs. Lockett tipped a candle over her letter, dribbling wax onto the back of the envelope. Then she pressed the wick of the candle into the soft puddle until it spread over the flap, extinguishing the flame and forming a seal.

"Gentlemen," she said, standing up, "we're turnin' in, but you're welcome to stay by the fire long as you want. Breakfast is at seven, all you can eat. Coffee'll be hot and strong. Come along, Minnie dear, you can finish your drawin' tomorrow —"

A sudden rattling of windows interrupted her. Wind whistled down the chimney and gusted under the front door. Rolly jumped up to roll a small rug against the draft. He cupped his face against a dark windowpane, looking outside.

"Ma," he said, "someone's coming."

Nessa looked out the window at a lantern bobbing along the path. Someone was walking toward the boarding-house, slowly against the blowing snow. In the distance she could see torchlight from the fort, half a mile away.

"Is it Papa?" asked Minnie. She looked at her mother with hope in her eyes.

"Oh, darlin', how I wish it was," said Mrs. Lockett. "But it's probably just a traveler. A stage was due this afternoon, but likely was late on account of the storm. Rolly dear" — she turned to her son — "run out there and greet the fellow with this lantern, but hurry, we don't want him gettin' lost. Snow's startin' to stick to the ground."

To Nessa she said, "Honey, would you put the kettle on, please? I reckon our visitor will need somethin' hot to drink."

Nessa was in the kitchen when the front door opened. She could hear Mrs. Lockett ushering the man to the fire and taking his cloak. Nessa remembered her own first night here. After days on a stagecoach she, too, had arrived in a storm, not knowing a soul, with no place to go. From Fort Larned, she had seen the lamplight at Mrs. Lockett's and set out with her valise. Nessa would never forget how warmly she was welcomed and cared for.

It was this memory that made Nessa smile. From the pantry she brought out what was left of the chocolate cake, a large half circle, enough for seven people. Then she set out plates, forks, and napkins. But as she was pouring a small pitcher of cream, a voice in the parlor caught her attention. Lowering herself to the bench, she listened.

Suddenly, she felt sick inside and light-headed. Her hands started shaking. The visitor wasn't a stranger after all.

Reverend McDuff had found her.

CHAPTER THREE

The Promise

*N*essa ran out onto the back porch. The cold took her breath. She knew she wouldn't be able to stay outside longer than a minute. How desperately she wanted to hide, to run far, far away, but she had already done that, trying to flee her arranged marriage with Reverend McDuff.

Now here he was. Tears of frustration stung her eyes. She felt fury at the man's stubborn insistence that they were to be husband and wife. His words from last April still haunted her: *The Lord told me you're to be my bride. I'll be good to you, dear, you'll see.*

Small drifts of snow were gathering in the corners of the porch. Nessa lifted her face to the wind. *What do I do now, Jesus?*

In the months since Nessa had lived in Prairie River, she had confided in only two people about why she had needed to escape the orphanage: Mrs. Lockett and her friend Ivy.

Upon hearing her story, Mrs. Lockett had made a promise. If Reverend McDuff followed Nessa out West, he would have to find room and board elsewhere in town.

But Nessa knew of the woman's compassion. She would not turn anyone away on a night like this.

As Nessa stood on the porch, she began shivering. Snowflakes chilled her neck. She rubbed her arms and stamped her feet while peeking in the kitchen window. Rolly was pulling out a chair near the stove for Reverend McDuff. But she could see only the minister's legs and boots as he stretched them toward the fire. Now the two gentlemen came in and were seating themselves at the long, oak table. Nessa saw they were chatting with the newcomer as if old friends.

Nessa felt sick with dread. She was too cold to pray and too cold to stay outside and avoid him any longer.

When she opened the door, all eyes turned toward her.

"Oh, there you are, honey." Mrs. Lockett came over and pressed her warm hands to Nessa's cheeks. "My word, you're freezing. What on earth were you doin' out there? Come meet our new pastor, all the way from . . . sir?" She looked at the visitor. "You didn't say the name of your town."

Reverend McDuff twisted around in his chair. "Why, that would be Independence, ma'am. Missoura. Hello there, Nessa."

Mrs. Lockett seemed surprised that he knew Nessa's name, then she nodded with understanding. "I see," she said. "Well, sir, tonight we're gonna make up a bedroll for you downstairs in the parlor. You'll be warm enough in front of the hearth." She squeezed Nessa's hand, then went to the table where she began slicing cake. She motioned to Minnie to pass around the plates.

"Then after breakfast," she continued, "my son here, Rolly, will take you into town. There's a new family offerin' room and board. I reckon that in trade for your preachin', the church committee will see that it don't cost you a cent."

"I'm grateful, ma'am," he said. "Thank you kindly."

Nessa watched Reverend McDuff, a man she'd known since she was four years old. He now was in his thirties with a thin mustache. Wisps of hair covered his balding head. As he talked with the others, he spoke in the low voice she remembered. Sitting through his sermons had been torture. He spoke so slowly, it had always seemed he was about to yawn. And because she rarely had seen him laugh or show emotion, Nessa found his face to be as bland as vanilla pudding.

And observing him now, he seemed the same. His smooth white hands passed the sugar to the other guests, then the cream. He was polite to everyone.

"Much obliged, ma'am," he said to Mrs. Lockett as she poured his tea. When Minnie set a plate of cake in front of him he said, "Why thank you, little girl. This looks mighty tasty." Then to Rolly he said, "And, young man, I appreciate your coming out on the path to meet me."

He kept glancing at Nessa as if he wanted to say something, but each time she looked away.

Some months ago she had received a letter from him.

But seeing the reverend's initials on the envelope, she had sent it back to him on the return stage, unopened. This rejection had infuriated him, according to Albert.

Sweet Albert. Her oldest friend from the orphanage was working at a newspaper in Independence. He had written to Nessa, warning of the minister's anger and his oath to come claim her as his rightful bride. Albert had pleaded with her not to marry Reverend McDuff, saying he himself would travel to Prairie River to protect her.

But why hadn't Albert come?

While the others climbed the stairs for their room, Nessa wiped the table, then swept the floor. By the light of a melting candle, Mrs. Lockett put away the dishes. In the parlor, Rolly unrolled a blanket onto the rug, in front of the fire.

"Here, Pastor," he said. "You can use my pillow."

Nessa wished everyone wasn't being so nice to Reverend McDuff! She wished he had made a raging scene so when others learned her story, they would understand why she didn't want to be near him. If only he had been arrogant or revealed his temper.

Instead, the minister behaved as a perfect gentleman. In the parlor he untied his boots, lined them up on the hearth, then settled under his blanket with a pleasant, "Good night, all!"

Nessa leaned her broom into the corner and hung the dustpan on its nail. She flinched when Mrs. Lockett touched her shoulder.

"My dear," she said, "no need for you to help with

breakfast tomorrow. Come down when you want." In the candlelight, the lines on her face looked soft. Her blue eyes regarded Nessa tenderly.

The tightness in Nessa's chest gave way to a sigh. With tears in her eyes she whispered, "Oh, Mrs. Lockett, he's ruining everything!" She hugged the woman, then ran upstairs.

CHAPTER FOUR

The Toast

At dawn, Nessa woke to the familiar sound of pots being moved over the iron stove. Ordinarily, she would be helping Mrs. Lockett. But today was different.

Without saying the words, the woman had let her know she did not have to face Reverend McDuff. At least not this morning.

Nessa closed her eyes. If only Albert were here. She pictured the last time she'd seen him — his mop of black curls and the affectionate way he gazed at her. Nessa had thought he had wanted to hold her hand, but she remembered how he had suddenly pulled away. It seemed he had just noticed his fingers were inky from the printing press. How fortunate he was to have been apprenticed to the *Missouri Daily Gazette*, even earning a small wage.

Upon their fourteenth birthdays, children at Mr. Carey's orphanage were expected to make their own way in the world. Albert was the lucky one. Nessa was told she must become a servant or marry Reverend McDuff.

Again Nessa wondered why her friend had not yet

come to Prairie River. In her mind she could see the Santa Fe Trail, how for miles and miles it cut across desolate land where only Indians and herds of buffalo roamed. It was dangerous country, but she wouldn't let herself consider the possibility that something might have happened to him.

As she lay in bed, she listened to the guests gathering downstairs, pushing chairs and benches up to the table, their voices praising Mrs. Lockett's good, strong coffee. Thankful for being able to linger under her snug buffalo robe, Nessa drew her knees up to her chest and relished the fur against her skin.

Nessa's bedroom was narrow with two small windows. One looked out over the wide, open prairie and the creek; the other looked toward the fort, which was the town everyone called Prairie River.

In the dim light she could see her breath. Her walls were dotted white from frost that clung to the nails. Nessa was glad she had slept with her clothes stuffed beside her, something she'd been doing since the first snowfall. Under the comfort of her fur and with a practiced wiggle, she removed her nightgown. Next to her in a warm lump was her camisole, which she pulled over her head, then a petticoat. Next came the blue dress Mrs. Lockett had given her for everyday wear, then woolen stockings.

As for her dress being rumpled, her long apron hid most of it and her sleeves were usually rolled up while doing chores. If Mrs. Lockett noticed the wrinkles, she never said.

The other warm lump beside Nessa this morning was her dog, curled into the corner by her pillow. Nessa stroked Green's yellow head.

"I smell sausage, girl," she said, "and maple syrup."

Green's eyes opened at the familiar tone. Her eyebrows moved left, then right, as she watched her mistress get out of bed to button her shoes. Nessa glanced in her mirror. She ran her fingers through her long auburn hair and tied it back with a ribbon. After breakfast she would brush and braid it properly.

When Nessa heard the kitchen door slam, she peered out her window. Rolly and Reverend McDuff were bundled up against the wind, heading for town. Snow was above their ankles as they made big steps, one behind the other, breaking the trail.

Relieved the minister was out of the house, she left her room. Green trotted ahead down the stairway and waited by the back door to be let outside.

"Good mornin', darlin'," said Mrs. Lockett. "Just sit yourself down next to Minnie." She put a plate of hot-cakes in front of Nessa. A chunk of melting butter slid over the edge of the cakes into a moat of syrup.

Nessa smiled up at her in appreciation. The two guests were at the table finishing their coffee. One of them lifted his cup toward Nessa, as if offering a toast.

"Here's to the bride," he said.

Nessa set her fork down. "Pardon me, sir?"

The man wiped his mustache with his napkin. "Well, miss," he said, "while we were all eating breakfast, the good reverend told us a little bit of this and a little bit of that, and how there's going to be a wedding soon."

Taking her spoon, Nessa dipped it into the sugar bowl, then stirred it in her tea. The room was quiet except for the spoon clinking against the porcelain cup. She forced herself to breathe slowly. She wanted to say something mean about the minister and tell her side of the story, but she didn't want to set a bad example for Minnie. Nor did she want to embarrass Mrs. Lockett.

At last, she looked up at the man. "Kind sir," she said, "I'm afraid you've been misinformed." Then she committed her fork to her hotcakes and began eating.

CHAPTER FIVE

Christmas Pies

All morning Nessa worked alongside Mrs. Lockett in the kitchen. She struggled to concentrate on the cutting and cooking of pumpkins that had been brought up from the cellar, but her mind kept replaying the events since last evening. There were so many things she wanted to say, but didn't know where to start.

She rolled out twelve piecrusts, then arranged them in pans on the table. While Mrs. Lockett held the large pot with a dish towel, Nessa ladled out pumpkin custard until all the tins were nearly full. The room had a buttery aroma with cinnamon and nutmeg.

"It's not fair," she finally blurted. "He's telling people that I ran off in the wee hours of our wedding day."

Mrs. Lockett returned the pot to the stove. "Well, dear, it's true, isn't it?"

Nessa felt stung by Mrs. Lockett's honesty. "But now everyone'll gossip," she said. "They'll think something's wrong with me because I don't want to marry him."

"Honey, hold your head high and don't doubt yourself just because the reverend's here with his nice manners and sad story. You're part of our family now, Nessa — I thank God for that — and you're also the best school-teacher Prairie River's ever had. As for other folks, well, there's not one blessed thing we can do about what they say or what they think."

Nessa savored Mrs. Lockett's words, wanting to hug her, but not wanting it to appear that she'd been desperate for a compliment. She looked at the pies. They would take several hours to bake because the wood-burning oven had space for just six at a time. She remembered harvesting the pumpkins with her students after a summer of tending their school garden. Every day the children had faithfully carried buckets of water from the creek. She was happy the results of their hard work could now be shared at the Christmas party. Being their teacher had brought Nessa more joy than she ever could have imagined.

She glanced at the clock on the kitchen wall. "Excuse me, Mrs. Lockett," she said, untying her apron, "I promised to visit Ivy this morning so we could plan the party, and it's almost eleven."

Mrs. Lockett laughed. "Then you best run along, darlin'. All that's left to do here is watch these ol' pies bake."

Freezing wind blew through Nessa's dress as she hurried along the snowy path to town. Green ran ahead of her. Though the air was cold, sunshine glistened off the drifts. She squinted against the glare, looking up at the blue canopy of sky. A pair of magpies flew overhead, squawking like jays.

Outside the perimeter of the fort were two sutlers' buildings, some distance apart. The first one Nessa came to was owned by Mr. Filmore, Ivy's father. They lived in a sod house behind the store. The compound also had a corral, a workshop, and a billiard hall for the soldiers. They had moved to Prairie River last spring, after Ivy's mother and sisters had died in a cholera epidemic.

"Come in!" called Ivy when Nessa knocked on the door.

The girl's braids were tied behind her shoulders with a blue ribbon that matched the bow on her plaid dress. She was bending to look in her oven.

"Papa got a bushel of pecans," she said to Nessa, "so he gave me some, but it took most of the morning to crack enough for these two pies."

Nessa was relieved to see the color in her friend's cheeks and that she was no longer spending the day in bed. Though Ivy had just recently recovered from typhoid and was often exhausted, her father said she could return to school in time for the Christmas party. Rolly would drive her in his wagon, wrapped warmly to protect her from the wind. He had converted his wagon into a sled by removing the wheels and attaching long, curved boards that could slide over the snow.

"Did you hear about the white girl living with Indians?" Ivy asked. "She's like us, Nessa, far from home and her mama is dead."

Nessa wanted to discuss the captive girl, but was distracted by her own worries. "Oh, Ivy, a new preacher came to town last night." She slumped into a chair by the stove. Green put a paw on Nessa's knee, her furry ears perked with concern.

Ivy's mouth dropped open. "Is he the one who —"

"Yes."

"Dear me." Ivy wrapped her arms around her friend. "Nessa, please don't run away again. Please."

"I hate him." Nessa was ashamed of her harsh words. "I mean, I hate it that he's come here. Things were beginning to go so well. He still believes the Lord said we're supposed to marry. He's telling everyone! Oh, Ivy." Nessa's eyes pleaded with her. "What if I've been wrong all these months? What if God's been trying to talk to me, but I haven't been listening? I feel so foolish right now . . . yet even so, in my heart I believe I shouldn't have to marry someone I don't love."

Ivy stroked Green's side. A moment passed. "Nessa, you have to believe in yourself. Ministers aren't perfect. Maybe because he likes you and he's lonely, he thinks that means God spoke to him."

Nessa was comforted by Ivy's friendship. Still, she was troubled. "Sunday is Christmas Eve," she said. "He'll probably be in church making friends with everyone. I can't bear to face him alone. Will you stay with me?"

"Like jam on bread," Ivy said.

CHAPTER SIX

—➤◆◄—

A New Student

The next day was Friday. Nessa stood in front of her students, seven in all. They looked at her expectantly, for today was their Christmas party. Their coats and mufflers were hung neatly in the entryway, and the schoolhouse was warm from the small iron stove in the center of the room.

Green lay in her usual spot, on an old blanket Rolly had brought for her bed. His horse, Buttercup, was sheltered in the barn constructed last month, a low sod building big enough to protect the animals on Sunday when townsfolk gathered here for church services.

Against a wall was a table with one of Ivy's pecan pies and one of Nessa's pumpkin pies. There was a basket filled with fried potatoes, thin and crispy with salt, and next to it a gallon jar of chocolate milk. Cups, plates, and forks were arranged on the red tablecloth.

The children kept glancing at the food.

"Our reading this morning is from Luke," Nessa began, "about the birth of Jesus." Last night in her bedroom she copied a page out of the large family Bible that had belonged to her father.

"And it came to pass in those days, that there went out a decree from Caesar Augustus, that all the world should be taxed. And this —"

A sudden gust of wind blew the paper from Nessa's hand as the door opened.

In walked a girl about her age, wearing a red wool cape with a red hat tied under her chin. Nessa thought she looked like Little Red Riding Hood, but didn't say so. She had never seen the girl before and did not want to risk offending her. Green got up from her bed to greet the visitor, tail wagging.

"Good morning," said Nessa. She smiled at the new student, then introduced the other children to her. "My name is Miss Nessa. And yours?"

"Mary Ellen Whipple," she said.

"Hello, Mary Ellen. You can sit in back with Ivy. We'll be having our party later this afternoon when we finish our lessons. You're most welcome to join us."

The girl looked around the room while hanging up her cape. She untied her hat, finding space for it by moving someone else's coat to another hook. Her dress was brown and cinched in at the waist by a corset. Red buttons were up to her chin and along her sleeves.

She turned to Nessa with her hands on her hips. "How old are you?" she asked.

Nessa was surprised by the question. "Fourteen," she answered.

Mary Ellen laughed. "Just as I thought. I'm older than you."

The children looked from the girl to their teacher. The room grew quiet, no shuffling of feet or whispers. Another gust of wind rattled the windows. Nessa bent down to retrieve her piece of paper, wondering what to do next. As teacher, she must remain calm and set a good example.

"Do you have any brothers or sisters?" Nessa asked the girl, trying to change the subject.

"Nope." Mary Ellen was still standing. "So how did you get a teaching certificate if you're only fourteen?"

Nessa's hands were behind her back, nervously fingering her skirt. Embarrassed by Mary Ellen's scrutiny, she tried to think of what to say. She didn't have a certificate, but did not know how to explain herself to a stranger, especially in front of her students.

Poppy raised her hand. Grateful for the interruption, Nessa called on the five-year-old.

"Miss Nessa, when our party starts, may we please play musical chairs?" Poppy's hair hung to her shoulders in reddish gold ringlets and her high-buttoned shoes were of fine leather, befitting an officer's daughter.

"I'll think about it, Poppy." Once again Nessa turned her attention to the new girl standing at the back of the classroom and decided to make another effort to get acquainted.

"You may be seated, Mary Ellen. Could you tell us what brought your family to Prairie River?"

Mary Ellen sat down. Smoothing her skirt, she stared at her lap. The students had turned in their seats to hear her answer. At last, she said, "My father said it was too crowded in Ohio, so here we are in this godforsaken wilderness. Come spring, he's going to plant corn and wheat, maybe buy some cattle. In the meantime we're taking in boarders. The new preacher is at our place, but then you probably already knew that."

Suddenly, Nessa's throat felt dry. Her cheerfulness from earlier had turned into a headache. Who knew what Reverend McDuff had told this family? She glanced at Ivy who was trying to encourage her with a smile. The others were watching her, too. Seeing their eager faces, Nessa decided to make an immediate change.

"Since this is our last day of school before Christmas," she said, "I think we should postpone our lessons until next week. The skies are clear, so let's have recess right now, then we'll celebrate — but be sure to bundle up warm before going outside."

An eruption of cheers and clamoring of shoes along the plank floor broke the tension. Green went to the door, then burst into a run when it was opened for her.

Nessa caught Mary Ellen by the elbow as she was reaching for her cape.

"Mary Ellen," she said, "would you like to come for tea tomorrow? At Mrs. Lockett's boardinghouse, say three o'clock? We can have a nice visit."

The girl shrugged Nessa off. "I'll think about it," she said, tying on her hat. "I'm going home now. This looks like a stupid party, anyway."

CHAPTER SEVEN

Mistletoe

On Saturday afternoon at three o'clock, Nessa stood at the kitchen window, waiting. The thermometer nailed to the back porch read twenty-nine degrees, and the sun was shining. She could see the effects of the wind, how it was wearing away the snow. Prairie grass showed through in patches.

"It's not too cold, and it's not snowing," Nessa said to Mrs. Lockett. She returned to the table to rearrange her plate of cookies. Water in the kettle was steaming. "I hope Mary Ellen comes. Guess I should wait to fill the teapot in case she comes, don't you think?" She bent down to pet Green who was sleeping by the stove.

"Yes, dear. That's a good idea."

Every few minutes Nessa looked out the window. She fingered the edge of the lace curtain.

"I don't think Mary Ellen likes me," she said. "I just wanted to make her feel welcome."

"Darlin', maybe she's busy helpin' her mother. As you know, there's always somethin' to cook or clean or fix when you take in boarders. Try to assume the best of a person, honey."

Nessa busied herself by dusting the bottles and jars in the pantry. She had hoped to make friends with Mary Ellen outside the classroom, where her students weren't listening to every word. She hadn't planned what to say, but since moving to Prairie River she had learned that people won't get to know you if you keep everything to yourself. From Ivy she had learned that to have a friend you must be a friend.

And she had also learned there were some people you didn't want as an enemy. She decided Mary Ellen was one of them.

At four o'clock, Nessa again went to the window. Seeing no one on the path, she covered the cookies with a cloth and set them on the shelf.

Mr. Filmore's store smelled of spices, smoked ham, and freshly ground coffee. The only hint of Christmas were the bundles of mistletoe his clerk had gathered from oak trees along the river. Ivy had tied red bows around the stems, put them in a basket, and written on a card, FIVE CENTS.

"They're selling fast," she said to Nessa when she came into the store with her dog. "A corporal's wife bought one and so did several laundresses. There're going to be all sorts of parties at the fort. Here, take one and hold it over your head — maybe a soldier will kiss you."

Color rose in Nessa's cheeks. She gave back the mistletoe. "I would never let a soldier kiss me."

Ivy gave a quick shrug. "I would," she said.

Nessa was shocked. "Really? But, Ivy, no one is courting you. Why would you kiss a stranger?"

Ivy nodded in the direction of three soldiers who stood at the counter talking to her father. Their blue wool coats were belted with shiny brass buckles and their buttons were polished to a shine. Golden epaulets adorned their shoulders. Two were clean-shaven, the other had a freshly trimmed beard. Their boots had left wet footprints on the floor. When they noticed the girls looking at them, they nodded respectfully.

Ivy leaned toward her friend and whispered, "Aren't they handsome? I love their uniforms."

Nessa glanced at the men but looked away. She hadn't had time to think about soldiers, though she admitted to herself that these three did look respectable. Then she recalled why she had come to the store in the first place.

"Ivy, remember how I invited the new girl to tea? Well, I waited an hour, but she never came."

"Huh. I wonder why?" said Ivy. "Maybe she got sick or had too many chores. Once my mother wouldn't let me go to a party because I spilled a coal bucket. It took hours to clean up."

"Yeah, probably something like that happened." Nessa was trying to do what Mrs. Lockett said, to think the best of Mary Ellen. But in her heart she believed the new girl had snubbed her. She was older than Nessa and probably smarter. She was sassy and wore a corset.

Maybe I should get a corset, she thought. Her beloved teacher at the orphanage, Miss Eva, had worn one. Miss

Eva also had twirled her hair atop her head. *Maybe I should start looking like a lady —*

Ivy shook her arm. "Nessa, I know what would cheer you up. A barn dance! Tonight at the Applewoods'."

"I don't know about that."

Mr. Applewood was the other sutler. He was also in charge of the school committee and had originally voted against Nessa's appointment, saying she was too young and unqualified to be a teacher. Whenever she came into his store, he and his wife were impatient with her and critical. She tried to avoid being near them.

"Ivy, maybe we could do something else. Besides, are you sure you're well enough to go out at night? It's the middle of winter."

"I don't care. All those weeks in bed made me think about things. Papa and the surgeon said I almost died. Now I want to get out and do things. Come on, Nessa. Go with me!"

Nessa looked at her friend. Freckles covered her nose and cheeks and the red ribbons in her braids gave her a cheerful appearance. Nessa hadn't heard her cough lately, so maybe the illness was completely gone. She wanted to help Ivy have fun.

"All right," said Nessa. "But just for a little while."

CHAPTER EIGHT

Barn Dance

After supper, Rolly and Nessa walked in the darkness to the sutler's compound, to pick up Ivy. He carried a lantern, which cast freckled light on the path in front of them. Snow crunched with their footsteps.

"I don't know how to dance," he said through the wool of his muffler.

Nessa patted her mittened hand on his shoulder. "Neither do I," she said. "We'll watch the others and learn that way. I've heard it's easy."

Rolly shook his head. "I don't know. I just hope you're right. Hey, there's Ivy looking out the window at us."

Mr. Filmore opened the door and invited them in while Ivy buttoned her coat.

"We'll take good care of her, sir," said Rolly. "At nine thirty, we'll leave the dance and bring her straight home. You don't have to worry about a thing."

As the three set out into the night they heard Mr. Filmore call through the wind, "Have fun!" Nessa looped arms with Ivy, holding her close. If her friend got sick again, she'd never forgive herself.

The Applewoods' barn was newly built with sod walls and a dirt floor, but no animals lived in it yet. The windows glowed with candlelight. Smoke swirling up from its chimney was whisked into the night.

Before they went inside, Rolly turned the wick down in his lantern and set it on a rock. He looked up at the cold sky where stars glistened like ice. The wind blew away the frost of his breath as soon as he spoke.

"Listen to me good," he said to the girls. "This is the first winter here for you two. Blizzards come up fast and mean. You can't see, period. If you start walking toward the house with your hands in front of you, but happen to drift off the path by a couple inches, you'll end up lost on the prairie, freezing to death. Happened last year to a couple of travelers staying with us. So don't leave the dance without me, is what I'm saying."

The barn was warm from a squat stove whose fire was fueled by dried buffalo droppings that had been gathered during summer. A table held a punch bowl with glasses and plates of pastries. In one of the corners were a fiddler, a guitarist, and a man playing the spoons. Their lively music provided a festive atmosphere. Several soldiers in crisp uniforms were gathered in conversation with some ladies of the fort who wore hoopskirts with elegant ruffles.

Nessa glanced around the room and was relieved that Reverend McDuff was not there.

Mrs. Applewood greeted the girls, pointing out hooks along the wall. "You can hang your coats over there." Then she turned her stern gaze to Nessa. "We expect appropriate behavior from our guests, or they'll be asked to leave."

Nessa knew Mrs. Applewood was speaking in general, but still her words stung. It felt as if the comment was directed at her personally, even though Nessa had thought relations with the Applewoods had been improving. She looked at the woman's narrow, pinched face and the tight bun atop her head, and wished she knew how to respond without starting a fight or spoiling the evening for Ivy. After all, it was nearly Christmas.

"Yes, ma'am," she said.

A boy in a clean white shirt approached Nessa and tipped his cap. Though he was only thirteen, he was taller than she was and broad across the shoulders from working on his father's ranch. His voice was husky.

"Miss Nessa," he said, "I know you're my teacher, but may I have the pleasure of this dance?"

"How nice, Howard. Thank you." Nessa felt herself blush. She had never danced and was unsure of herself. When he rested his hand at her waist and led her to the center of the room, she felt uncomfortable at his touch.

But soon enough she forgot her nervousness as Big Howard stepped gracefully around the floor, guiding her with steady arms. She was surprised by his gentleness because he was the student who had given her so much trouble her first term.

By their second dance, Nessa was beginning to enjoy

herself. She was glad she had worn the scarlet dress Mrs. Lockett had sewn for her. Its long sleeves had black piping around the wrists, and the collar cupped her chin. Nessa glanced down for a peek at her new shoes. Given to her by Ivy, they were of soft black leather that buttoned from her instep to above her ankle. She swung her foot a bit, just to see the lacy hem of her petticoat.

There was no mirror in the barn to catch her reflection, but she thought that perhaps her hair looked nice tonight because she had woven a scarlet ribbon into the braid. Nessa felt fancy even though she wasn't wearing earrings or a necklace.

When the third dance began, Rolly tapped Big Howard on the shoulder. "May I?" he asked Nessa.

She smiled, enjoying the attention and also the sight of Rolly's hair. He had combed it tonight, but still it stuck up straight like hay. "Yes," she laughed. "Let's."

"I still don't know what I'm doin'," Rolly said, "but here goes!" When he offered his arm with a tug, Nessa laughed again. It didn't matter that they kept bumping into each other. She felt pleasure from the music and from being among so many people having fun. Trying to dance with Rolly made her feel lighthearted and joyous. She turned her head, looking for Ivy, to see if she, too, was enjoying herself.

When she finally caught sight of her friend, she couldn't believe her eyes.

At the doorway, a soldier was helping Ivy put on her wrap. Before Nessa could do anything, Ivy took the man's hand and walked outside with him.

CHAPTER NINE

══╼•◆•╾══

The Gray Curtain

"**W**e have to stop her," Nessa said to Rolly, pulling away from him. She hurried through the crowd to find her coat, then rushed out the door.

The night was black except for squares of yellow light coming from the windows of the fort. Stars were strewn across the sky, down to the horizon like a long, speckled drape. *Good,* she thought, *no clouds.*

She looked in every direction but didn't see anyone.

"Ivy!" she called into the night. As she searched the blackness, Nessa worked at buttoning her coat, pulling up its collar to cover her neck. The wind numbed her skin. She was worried because Ivy had left with a soldier she had met only an hour before, but most of all, Nessa worried that her friend might become ill again being out in the cold.

Jesus, she prayed, *please protect Ivy. Help us find her.*

Rolly joined Nessa and held up his lantern. Light cast a circle around them. "Ivy, where are you?" he called.

It was too cold to wander around the Applewoods'

34

compound, and it was dark. Out the corner of her eye she noticed a light suddenly go out. But looking up, she realized a section of stars had disappeared. She grabbed Rolly's sleeve to get his attention, then pointed to the sky.

Clouds. And they were moving fast.

"We have to hurry," he said.

"Where could they be?" Nessa asked, realizing most of the town's buildings were dark. Something wet touched the side of her nose. A snowflake.

Rolly's lantern illuminated a path leading to the Applewoods' shed. Not sure where else to go, they followed it to a small stone building that stood against a backdrop of starlight. Even through the wind, Nessa could hear a man's voice, then the giggle of a girl.

She and Rolly crept forward, stepping into the doorway. The soldier was silhouetted against the pale opening of a window. He was leaning forward to kiss Ivy.

Nessa felt awkward seeing such intimacy, but when she heard Ivy cough, concern overcame her. Without thinking, she rushed toward her friend.

"Ivy," she cried, "you can't be out in this weather. You'll get sick." Nessa grabbed her arm and pulled her away. Rolly took the girl's other arm.

The wind had become sharper with cold. Snowflakes pricked Nessa's cheeks. She did not want to return to the party because Mrs. Applewood would notice their distress and cause a scene.

"Please don't tell Papa," Ivy begged.

"Hurry," said Nessa. She was angry and scared and

cold and did not feel like making a promise right now. She and Rolly ushered Ivy toward the light of her father's house.

Snow was falling fast, stinging her eyes. Nessa tried to keep sight of the distant candlelight in Mr. Filmore's kitchen, but blowing snow was dimming it by the second. Step by step, she concentrated on not getting lost.

Rolly pounded on Mr. Filmore's door, and once Ivy was safely inside, he took Nessa's hand and led her away.

"We can't stay," Rolly shouted. The wind flapped his muffler against his face. "Come on, Nessa."

They could see Mrs. Lockett's boardinghouse, which was about a half mile away. Lights blazed in the windows upstairs and down, but snow was putting a gray curtain between them. Wind screamed in her ears. Nessa felt panicky when the house vanished from sight altogether, then reappeared as a faint blur.

"Hurry," cried Rolly, now running, pulling her along.

Nessa looked behind her at the sky. The blackness moved toward them like a shadow, swallowing the stars, one by one. Her lungs hurt from gulping the frozen air, but she ran with Rolly, the lantern swinging at his side.

When she saw Mrs. Lockett standing in the open doorway, golden light surrounding her and spilling out onto the porch, she choked back a sob of relief, not allowing herself to cry.

CHAPTER TEN

Waiting Out the Storm

The storm howled through the night. On the morning of Christmas Eve, Nessa stepped from under her buffalo robe to look out her window. Wind gusted between small cracks at the sill where there lay a dusting of snow. She could see nothing but white and gray swirling beyond the glass.

Smiling to herself, she crawled back into bed to get dressed. It was Sunday, but there would be no services in this weather. Church was held in the schoolhouse, which was on the open prairie, a ten-minute walk from Mrs. Lockett's. By now, Nessa realized how dangerous it was to set out during a blizzard. She was thankful Rolly brought her — and Ivy — safely home and thankful for another week that she could put off facing Reverend McDuff.

As she fumbled for her pile of clothes, she thought about the dance last night and how good it felt to glide around the room to music. Rolly and Big Howard had led Nessa along the dance floor with such certainty that even now she felt warm with the memory.

At breakfast, only Rolly and Minnie sat at the table with Nessa, no boarders. During winter, few traveled the Santa Fe Trail because of storms that could rise on the vast prairie. Fort Larned was one of a string of outposts west of the Missouri River, most separated by a one- or two-day ride. Nessa knew that ever since Captain Lockett had gone to war in the East, Mrs. Lockett had depended on travelers to pay her for room and board.

"With the Lord's help, we'll manage just fine," she told Nessa as she sat down with her coffee. "Autumn was busy, so I tucked away a few dollars, filled the pantry and our cellar. Now, my dear ones, tomorrow's Christmas. If this storm keeps up, I reckon it'll just be the four of us. What shall we have for our special dinner?"

Nessa brushed some bread crumbs off the table into her palm, then onto her empty plate. She had been thinking about Ivy's eagerness to be kissed and wondered what she felt about the soldier. Who was he, anyway? And why had he been so forward with Ivy? She had been coughing when Nessa found her, and this thought continued to trouble Nessa. What if being out in the cold had caused a relapse? Nessa wished the blizzard would stop so she could visit her friend, but on the other hand, she was thankful church had been canceled.

"What's that you're thinkin' about, darlin?" Mrs. Lockett asked her. She turned up the wick on the oil lamp. Its glass chimney filled with light and reflected off the ceiling, dispelling the gloom of the storm. Heat from the oven brought the aroma of baking bread.

Nessa didn't want to mention Ivy and the soldier, especially in front of Minnie.

"Oh . . . the party," she said. "Howard and Rolly both asked me to dance. And I did!"

Mrs. Lockett patted her hand. "That's my girl, Nessa."

Rolly tied a rope to the back porch railing and, holding it in his mittened hand, stepped into the blizzard. Nessa watched his back disappear in the blowing snow as he went to feed Wildwing and the other animals. As soon as he bumped into the barn, he would fasten the rope to a post so he could find his way back to the house. Then this evening it would be Nessa's turn to do the same. She looked forward to petting her horse and talking to him.

In the meantime she helped Mrs. Lockett scrub the kitchen floor, then dust the high corners for cobwebs.

"Darlin', that's enough work for now," Mrs. Lockett said. "Take some time for yourself."

Nessa watched out the back window. When at last she saw the dark shape of Rolly safely returning from the barn, she allowed herself to go upstairs. Though her room was cold, it was cozy. Sitting on the edge of her bed, she wrapped the buffalo robe around her shoulders, Green curled up at her side.

She opened her trunk. It was green-and-red-striped, made of tin with exquisite silver corners and a silver latch. She would be forever grateful to Miss Eva for discovering it in the attic of the orphanage and sending it to Prairie River.

In it, Nessa found her father's Bible and her mother's devotional. Among other treasures, there were clues from her early childhood, before she had been orphaned — bundles of letters, drawings in her mother's hand, clothing, and assorted small boxes holding trinkets that still remained a mystery to Nessa.

From her father's notes in the Bible, she had learned that her mother died after giving birth to twins. There was no death notice for the babies, so Nessa assumed they survived and, if still alive, would be ten years old. A boy and a girl or two girls or two boys? Her father hadn't said. She had no other clues about her siblings. She was tempted to again write Aunt Britta in Wisconsin, someone she knew only from the dated letters. Maybe she would have some answers for Nessa.

Green worked her way under the fur where her mistress could pet her. Nessa stroked the dog's head, staring at the solid white window. She tried to imagine her siblings. How wonderful it would be if there were also grandparents, uncles, and cousins.

Then a thought occurred to her. Nessa didn't know if her aunt Britta had received her letter or if she was even still alive. But if she was and if the woman were to write saying that there was indeed family, Nessa would be overjoyed.

It would mean that if Nessa left Prairie River to be with relatives, no one could say she was again running away from Reverend McDuff.

CHAPTER ELEVEN

―――◈―――

Mr. Button's News

$\mathcal{N}$essa awoke Christmas morning to silence. The wind had stopped. A thin ray of sunlight lay across her bed. Just as she sat up, Minnie burst into her room.

"Nessa, hurry. Come downstairs. Look what's on the table." Minnie rushed to Nessa, her small arms hugging her tight. "We don't have to get dressed because there's no one here but us. Come on!"

Green bounded downstairs, followed by the girls. Nessa was surprised to see Mrs. Lockett at the stove because the house had been so quiet. She hadn't realized she had slept so late. The warm kitchen had an aroma of cinnamon and sausage. Four places were set at the table. At each one was a package wrapped in newspaper with a red ribbon. There was a bowl of tiny orange balls.

"They're real oranges," said Mrs. Lockett. "The priest from the Taos pueblo brought 'em a few weeks ago when he stayed with us, said they were grown in California. I've been savin' 'em special for today."

Cold air entered the kitchen as Rolly came in from the porch carrying an armful of kindling and buffalo chips.

"It's all dry," he said, "thanks to the tarpaulin. 'Morning, Nessa. Your first Christmas here in Prairie River, ain't that grand?"

"Oh, yes," she said.

"Mother," he continued, "I saw Mr. Button on his sleigh, heading to town from his ranch. I reckon he'll stop by on his way home, like he usually does."

"Then I'll get the coffee going," she said.

Nessa dashed upstairs to put on her blue dress because she didn't want to be in her nightgown when company came. She also wanted to bring out her gifts for the Locketts. In her trunk last night she had found an ivory-handled penknife that must have belonged to her father. She had tied it up in a scrap of calico for Rolly. For Minnie there was a charcoal pencil and small sketch pad. And for Mrs. Lockett, a teacup.

Not only was it Nessa's first Christmas in Prairie River, it was the first time she remembered celebrating it with a family. A quiet excitement stirred within her.

During breakfast, Minnie's impatience for everyone to open their presents made Mrs. Lockett laugh.

"All right, dear," she said. "Your papa would approve. How he loves the fun of Christmas morning."

But a jingling of sleigh bells drew their attention to the window. There came Mr. Button up the lane, his horses breaking a path in the fresh snow.

Rolly grabbed his coat from the hook and ran outside to help cover the team with their blankets to keep them warm.

"Merry Christmas," cried Mr. Button from the porch, stamping snow off his feet as he came inside. He hung up his coat and cap, then smoothed his mustache, which was bushy and curled onto his cheeks. Suspenders held up his trousers over his large stomach. On his shirt were assorted stains from past meals. "Such a fine day. Lookie here, Minnie, I got something for you."

The man reached deep into his pocket. He handed her a small rag doll made from a sock. String shaped the arms, legs, and a head, which had yellow yarn for hair. Tiny blue buttons were eyes, red embroidery formed a smiling mouth. "Sewed 'er myself, honey, just for you."

"Oh, thank you, Mr. Button. She's perfect, I love her."

The tips of Mr. Button's fingers were black with ink from his printing press. He was editor of the *Prairie River Journal.* The newspaper office was at the fort, but he lived outside town with his younger cousin, Hoss. The school was on a section of their ranch, so the cousins saw to its upkeep. By the time Nessa and her students arrived each morning, the room was already warm from the fire the men had started earlier. They did the same for church on Sundays.

Mr. Button sat in his usual spot at the table as Mrs. Lockett poured his coffee. He added some milk, took a sip, then nodded with appreciation. "Still the best in town, Vivian," he said to her. "Strong and hot, just how I like it."

Nessa smiled because he always said that. She sliced into the pan of frosted cinnamon rolls, scooped one onto a plate, and passed it to him. Mr. Button winked at her.

"Thank you, my dear." He and Nessa had first become acquainted on the stagecoach from Missouri to Prairie River. They were passengers with Fanny Jo and Laura, sisters who now lived on Suds Row with the laundresses. Nessa was always comforted by Mr. Button's presence and pleased that he and the sisters lived nearby. Because of their journey west, the four of them shared a little more history than they did with the townsfolk, even if only by a couple of weeks.

"How's your day going, Mr. Button?" asked Nessa.

"Good news, bad news," he answered.

"Oh?" said Mrs. Lockett. She set down the coffeepot and regarded him with concern.

He shook his head. "A wolf's been coming around, didn't think too much about it except this morning when we let the stock out into the corral and he jumped over the fence and bit our little mule, Betty. I could've touched him, he was that close to me, but he ran away before Hoss could get a shot off."

Mr. Button paused to cut a bite of cinnamon roll, then forked it into his mouth. The kitchen was quiet except for the sound of him swallowing.

"See, wolves hunt in packs, that's what they do. Ain't normal for a wolf to be off by himself or getting close to humans. Not normal a-tall."

"D'you mean he's sick?" asked Rolly. "Could it be rabies?"

Mr. Button shrugged his shoulders. "Hoss and I couldn't be sure without getting a better look at him. We didn't want to take a chance with poor Betty — there's no cure for rabies and the dying part is just terrible — so we went ahead and put her down. And on Christmas, of all days. That's one of the reasons I'm here, to warn folks about a wolf being on the loose."

Minnie hugged her doll to her chest. "Poor ol' Betty," she said. "But, Mr. Button, what's the good news?"

He raised his eyebrows, which were as bushy as his mustache. "Well, honey," he said, "with the sleighs, Hoss and I tramped a pretty good path from the schoolhouse to town. We've got a small fire going, so by noon it'll be warm enough for a worship service. How I love Christmas. We'll sing carols and get to hear our new preacher. I believe you folks already met Reverend McDuff?"

Suddenly, Nessa felt sick inside. While the others answered yes, she excused herself and went upstairs. She wouldn't have a week of peace after all. Noon was just three hours away.

CHAPTER TWELVE

———≫·◆·≪———

Christmas Day

Ivy sat in the last row beside Nessa, their arms touching. Green lay at their feet. Teaching school, Nessa was always up by the blackboard, but during church she preferred to be where people couldn't stare at her.

The room was cozy from the fire and crowded with her students, their families, and several soldiers. Sunlight streamed in through the south-facing windows that revealed a snowy landscape. The view reminded her that the girl living with Indians still hadn't been rescued. Suddenly, she felt grateful. Even though Nessa was uneasy being here, at least she was inside where it was warm and her best friend was at her side.

Mr. Filmore stood in front. "Welcome, everyone," he said, smiling at friends and townsfolk. His vest was made from colorful patches of cloth, which had been sewn by Ivy, and he wore a black string tie. Since September, Prairie River had been without a minister so he, Mr. Button, and some of the other men had been taking turns each Sunday, reading scripture and giving a devotional.

This afternoon when he introduced Reverend McDuff,

he motioned toward the Whipple family, acknowledging them as the generous folks who were housing the minister. Mary Ellen was in the front row. Her dress had puffed sleeves with layers of lace around the wrists and a high, frilly collar. She turned around to look at Nessa with a smirk.

Mary Ellen's expression made Nessa so uncomfortable, she felt prickly.

To make matters worse, Reverend McDuff was walking around the room, nodding to people, and greeting them with his pleasant manners. Every time he tried to catch Nessa's attention, she looked away. She wished she could escape out onto the cold prairie, where she would run and run.

Feeling miserable, Nessa closed her eyes. *How can this be, Lord? I'm sorry for being irritated, especially on Christmas, but why did he have to come and why won't he understand?*

Her prayer was interrupted by the soft strum of a guitar. Hoss was up front. Though just nineteen, he was taller and broader than his cousin, Mr. Button. His hair stood up straight like bristles on a brush.

"Folks," he began, "on account of our hymnals being burned in the fire last summer, I picked songs that most everyone knows by heart. Children, you're first. Come on up here."

A rustling filled the room as boys and girls left their parents to walk up by the blackboard. Poppy stood on her tiptoes to wave to Nessa, then so did Augusta and Lucy. Nessa smiled at them, comforted by their cheerfulness.

Younger children held their older siblings' hands, squirm-
ing with shyness.

"Ready?" Hoss asked them, playing the first chord. He
smiled at them. "One and two and . . ."

Silent night, holy night!
All is calm, all is bright
Round yon Virgin Mother and Child.
Holy infant so tender and mild,
Sleep in heavenly peace,
Sleep in heavenly peace.
Silent night, holy night!
Shepherds quake at the sight;
Glories stream from heaven afar,
Heavenly hosts sing Al–le–lu–ia;
Christ, the Savior, is born!
Christ, the Savior, is born!

At the sound of their young voices, Nessa felt choked
up. She remembered Miss Eva teaching her this song
when she was four years old and new to the orphanage.
During the day when Nessa was with her teacher or
playing in the yard with Albert, she was fine. But late at
night when the house was dark and everyone in bed,
Nessa would be desperate with loneliness. She would cry
into the sleeve of her nightgown, hoping no one would
hear, and whispering the words to this song — *Silent
night, holy night . . . Christ, the Savior, is born.*

When she would awaken the next day feeling comforted, a small seed of faith began to grow in her. She had felt and believed Jesus was by her side.

Now Nessa yearned more than ever for that comfort. Everything seemed so upside down. She continued to pray in her heart, *Lord, please help me be nice to Mary Ellen and show me what to do about Reverend McDuff.*

The children clamored back to their seats as Hoss began playing "O Come, All Ye Faithful." Everyone joined in, finishing with "Joy to the World! The Lord Is Come." When the room again grew quiet, Reverend McDuff took his Bible up front and faced his new congregation.

"Merry Christmas," he said in his slow voice. His pale mouth barely moved. "Thank you one and all for your warm welcome. Now . . ." He began thumbing the pages of scripture.

Nessa felt her eyes grow heavy. The next thing she knew, he said, "Amen," and there was a noise of benches scraping across the floor. Had she really fallen asleep? The sermon was over. People were getting out of their seats and beginning the fellowship.

CHAPTER THIRTEEN

Church Supper

As tables were being arranged inside the schoolhouse, Nessa helped set out the pies and food platters that the women had brought in their picnic baskets. She hoped there would be a quiet moment when she could talk to Ivy about the soldier. She had so many questions! But as the moments passed, she grew uneasy knowing Reverend McDuff was in the same room, trying to catch her eye. It would be impossible to keep avoiding him.

At last, she decided there was something she must do.

While everyone was busy eating, Nessa worked her way through the crowd to the entryway where the coats were hung. The minister was seated on a bench, talking with Hoss.

Her heart was racing when she approached them. "Excuse me," she said, "may I please have a word with you, Reverend?"

He blinked as if startled. The slightest of smiles creased his cheeks. "Why, certainly," he said. He patted the seat next to him, but Nessa remained standing.

"Guess I'll be going back for seconds now," said Hoss as he left with his plate.

Nessa watched Hoss walk toward the tables. Now more than ever, she truly felt alone. Even Green was on the other side of the room, watching for dropped food.

"Vanessa dear," the minister said, "it's so good to see you again. When you left Independence, Mr. Carey and I were rather concerned —"

"Reverend McDuff," said Nessa. "Please stop telling people that you and I are getting married." She could feel her insides shaking. Her throat had gone dry, making her words feel like wool in her mouth.

"Whatever do you mean?" He stood up. Gravy dripped from his plate onto the floor.

Nessa felt her courage failing. How could she tell a man of God that she believed he was mistaken about some things? Especially now, surrounded by people who automatically trusted him because he was their pastor. As much as she disliked his way of thinking, she didn't want to embarrass him. She looked down at her shoes.

"What I mean," she said, unable to meet his gaze, "is that I'm not going to marry you."

"Vanessa." His voice was firm. "I believe you're to be my bride and that I'm to take care of you. We'll be happy together, you'll see. The Lord told me."

Her mind raced with thoughts. Knowing people were watching them made her neck feel hot. Leaning close enough to whisper, she said, "But . . . the . . . Lord . . . didn't . . . tell . . . me."

The minister's face turned red and his jaw tightened. "Good heavens, you're much too young to presume that God Almighty would speak to you. Are you trying to spoil Christmas for everyone?"

Voices in the room dropped to a murmur. From the corner of her eye she noticed Mary Ellen watching her.

Nessa felt trapped. She could feel her heart thumping as if she had just run a race. She didn't know how to explain about her prayers or how when she read the Bible it seemed as though God indeed was speaking to her. Certainly she hadn't heard the Lord's voice through her ears, but she believed she heard Him with her heart and with her mind.

"I'm not going to marry you," she repeated, reaching behind him for her coat. "Green, come here, girl." Nessa gave a quick whistle through her teeth, then stepped out into the cold.

Outside, Nessa crunched along the path that Mr. Button's horses had made. Snow clung to her hem and came in over the tops of her shoes. Green ran ahead, then circled back to keep her mistress in sight. The sun was so bright Nessa shaded her eyes with her hand.

"Nessa . . . wait!"

She turned to see Rolly running toward her. His cheeks were red from the wind.

"You shouldn't ever walk alone in winter," he called. "It's too dangerous. And now there's that wolf."

The wolf. Nessa had forgotten about it.

When Rolly caught up to her, he gave a playful tug to her braid. They were both wearing the beautiful plush scarves Mrs. Lockett had knit them for Christmas. His was red, hers royal blue. They were wide enough to cover their heads and wrap around their necks.

"I heard what you told the new minister, Nessa. Everyone did."

Nessa sighed. Her breath made frost between them. "Rolly, I hope you'll understand."

"Oh, I do, Nessa. You said you don't want to marry him. I understand fine. He seems decent enough. Anyhow," said Rolly, "let's surprise Mother by cooking supper for her tonight. I invited the sisters, also Hoss and Mr. Button."

Rolly's enthusiasm made Nessa smile. She wanted to touch the blond wisps of hair that stuck out from his cap. Instead, she punched his arm.

"Race you!" Nessa lifted her skirt and took off running, big steps through the snow. When Green saw the game, she began barking with excitement and raced figure eights between the two.

High above them, blue sky reached to the far horizons. The prairie was white and vast. Along the river, the leafless trees glistened with icicles. In the distance was the fort where curls of smoke rose from chimneys, and the flag that stood one hundred feet above the parade ground was flapping in the wind.

CHAPTER FOURTEEN

The Wolf

Later Christmas afternoon, Nessa parted the kitchen curtain to look out, excited that the sisters were coming for supper. Ever since she had nearly ruined their friendship by gossiping, she was grateful they were no longer angry with her. Things were as sweet as their first days together on the stagecoach. Also, Fanny Jo was now expecting a baby.

But as Nessa watched the trail, she heard a gunshot echo through the wind. Her heart quickened.

"Rolly?" Her voice was strained. "Fanny Jo and Laura were supposed to be here by now."

"I'll get the sled," he said, fastening his coat. When Nessa saw him take the rifle down from its rack over the door, she knew his fears matched her own.

Hoss said, "I'm comin' with you."

"Me, too," said Mr. Button. They were hurrying down the steps of the porch before Nessa could tell them to be careful.

Her stew simmered on the stove and the biscuits Rolly had earlier spooned onto a pan were baking. Nessa ran upstairs. From the hallway, she could see into Mrs. Lockett's bedroom where she and Minnie were wrapping a present together. Nessa didn't want to alarm them. Unnoticed, she slipped into her room to get a better view from her window.

The prairie looked pale in the waning sunlight. Thin shadows stretched behind snowdrifts that were rippled like waves at sea. From her other window, Nessa watched Rolly snap the reins of his sled, urging Buttercup to hurry, the cousins riding alongside on their horses. They disappeared around a bend in the trail, then a moment later reappeared on a rise that turned toward town.

Mrs. Lockett sat at the table listening to the sisters, trying to console them.

"And to think it's Christmas," Laura said, in tears. "Those poor men."

"Now, now." Mrs. Lockett handed the girl a cup of hot tea. "Maybe they'll be all right. The fort has a fine surgeon."

Fanny Jo shook her head, wiping her wet cheeks with her handkerchief. She was nineteen, one year older than her sister. "I don't think so, Mrs. Lockett," she said. "Laura and I saw the wolf up close. It was bigger than any dog and skinny, as if it was sick. We had just left Suds Row and were walking past the barracks. When it crept toward us, some soldiers shouted and ran at it, but just as they drew pistols and fired, it went right for them instead. We ran and that's when we saw Rolly with his sled."

"I shot at it like this," said Rolly, demonstrating with

his arms and squinting. "But only got its paw. It left blood in the snow when it ran off. The soldiers shot, too, but it looked like their bullets just grazed its fur. Everything happened so fast. One man was bit in the leg, the other was bleeding from his neck."

At this, Fanny Jo burst into tears again. "How dreadful," she said, struggling to compose herself. "I'm sorry, it's just so upsetting. Those soldiers were only trying to help us. What if the wolf has rabies?" She leaned back in her chair to catch her breath and rest her hand upon her large middle. Her baby was due any day now. Her husband, a lieutenant, was stationed at Fort Dodge.

The back door opened. Hoss came in the kitchen with a lantern and the aroma of the pipe he was smoking. His brown woolen shirt was clean, in honor of Christmas, and his suspenders red. He wore a bow tie, bright blue.

"Well," he said, setting his pipe on the table, "the horses and cow are calm, sure enough. Me and Button checked around the barn and henhouse, made sure all the doors were latched good and tight, he's there now spreading fresh hay. There're no prints in the snow, Mrs. Lockett, so maybe the wolf is long gone."

"Lord, I hope so. I surely do thank you for checkin' again, Hoss."

When everyone was seated, Nessa dished up bowls of stew. Minnie had set the table with a plate of sweet pickles that had been made last summer with cucumbers from the garden. Hot biscuits and butter were passed around, and there was a pitcher of fresh, frosty milk that had been cooling on the porch. Green took her usual position under the table where she could lick up any spills.

Mrs. Lockett's eyes creased as she smiled at her friends. Then she folded her hands and bowed her head. *"Dear Jesus, You were born in a stable all those years ago and now here we are celebrating that day again. From the bottom of my heart, I thank You for this food and for everyone gathered here tonight. Lord, bless their faraway families and bless my Charlie in that hospital back East. Please bring him home to us soonly. And, Lord, we ask you to take care of those two soldiers that were bit by the wolf. Thank You, Jesus. Amen."*

Nessa picked up her knife and reached for the butter. Considering the events with the wolf, her own troubles seemed small. Recalling her conversation with the minister, she felt relief from a great burden. She continued praying silently. *Lord, please give me the strength to go to church on Sundays, and I'm sorry ahead of time if I make a mistake and am mean to him, which is how I feel whenever —*

"Nessa, dear girl," said Hoss, "would you like for me to pass you a biscuit? That small, round thing you're buttering is my tobacco pouch."

CHAPTER FIFTEEN

———◆———

A Long Night

After supper, Rolly brought his sled from the barn so he could take the sisters home. Stars were beginning to appear in the darkening sky, and along the western horizon there was still a splash of pink from the setting sun. The wind was cold. It blew Buttercup's mane off her neck and rattled branches from the lilac bushes by the back porch. Everyone came outside to yell "Merry Christmas" one more time. Hoss and Mr. Button were on their horses, holding their lanterns high, ready to escort the group.

As Fanny Jo stepped onto the runner, she suddenly doubled over. She grabbed the edge of the seat with her gloved hand as she slid to the ground.

"Dear me," she gasped.

Laura screamed her sister's name.

Hoss jumped from his horse, handing Rolly the reins and his lantern. "Allow me, madam," he said, lifting Fanny Jo in his arms and carrying her up the steps and back into the house.

Rolly and Nessa dragged a straw mattress from one of the upstairs guest rooms down to the parlor. Mr. Button built up the fire to make the room warm, then left with his cousin to find the doctor.

Nessa made the bed with fresh linens and helped Fanny Jo out of her heavy wool smock. Dressed now in just a slip and camisole, she eased herself down to lie on her side.

Mrs. Lockett ushered Rolly into the kitchen. "Fanny Jo will be needin' privacy now, son, but we still could use your help. Seein' as how we might be up into the wee hours, can you please make sure we don't run out of firewood or chips and also keep watch over the stove? We'll need plenty of hot water."

"Yes, Ma."

Minnie looked at both of them with a worried expression. "Did the wolf hurt Fanny Jo?" she asked.

"No, darlin'," said her mother. "She's about to have her baby, is all. She's nearly a week overdue. Can you help by keepin' the kitchen tidy? And if anyone's hungry, there's fresh bread on the warming rack that you can slice up with some cheese. That's my big girl."

The night wore on. Nessa ached to hear Fanny Jo's increasing cries of pain. She remembered how she had been with the blacksmith's wife, Mrs. Bell, early last summer, when she went into labor. The baby had been born during a thunderstorm, on the floor of the schoolhouse. The sisters had been there, too.

And Peter. How he had marveled at the tiny infant. Who could have possibly imagined that days later the six-year-old boy would die from the bite of a rattlesnake?

But Nessa forced herself not to dwell on the sorrow she still felt. She put a cool cloth on Fanny Jo's forehead, then took her hand.

"Fanny Jo," she said. "Remember that storm with Mrs. Bell, when you, Laura, and I were there?"

The young woman nodded. Her breathing was too labored for her to speak.

"And remember that pretty baby boy she held in her arms when it was over?"

Another nod.

"Well, Fanny Jo, soon enough you'll have your own pretty baby to hold. You'll see. And we'll stay right here with you."

Nessa bolted awake in her chair. When she realized the clock on the mantel was chiming seven, she was ashamed of herself for falling asleep. Already it was morning. In the dim light, she saw an exhausted Mrs. Lockett at the bedside and could hear Fanny Jo groan. Laura lay on the floor, holding her sister's hand. Green was curled beside them, her head on Fanny Jo's foot.

Nessa noticed Laura was crying.

Taking Nessa aside, Mrs. Lockett said, "We don't know why the doctor ain't come yet, but I wish to high heaven he would hurry. I think we're losing her."

CHAPTER SIXTEEN

⟫•◆•⟪

The Warming Rack

Nessa knelt beside Fanny Jo, putting her ear to the swollen abdomen. She waited and listened. The only sounds she could hear were from the fireplace — a hiss from the glowing embers — and the rhythmic ticking of the clock.

Then against her cheek, she felt the slightest of movements. With a gentle touch, she pressed her hand there and again felt something move. Nessa felt a rush of hope and energy.

"Can you hear me, Fanny Jo?" asked Nessa.

"Yes," she whispered. The young woman's lips were dry, her skin warm. As she had seen Mrs. Lockett do, Nessa gave Fanny Jo a spoonful of water, then when she swallowed, another.

"I can feel your baby kicking, Fanny Jo. Are you tired?" She nodded.

"Remember how Mrs. Bell took deep breaths, how she pushed hard to help the baby be born? Can you do that, Fanny Jo? I'll hold your hand. Laura's right here, and so is Mrs. Lockett."

After a long moment Fanny Jo let out a shuddering cry, then a scream.

Nessa felt chills up her spine. She wanted to pray, but was lost for words. "Jesus, please help. . . ." was all she said.

Another scream.

"That's my girl, Fanny Jo," said Mrs. Lockett. "Not too much longer. Keep tryin', darlin'."

Nessa noticed Rolly in the kitchen. He was holding his little sister on his lap, his arms wrapped around her. Minnie's face was twisted with tears, and she was trying to look in the parlor. Seeing their distress upset Nessa even more.

A sharp squeeze to her hand returned her attention to Fanny Jo. Another scream came, then a gasp of relief.

Mrs. Lockett held up what looked like a small gray doll. "A boy," she said in a soft voice. She cut its umbilical cord with a knife, knotted it, then wrapped the infant in a towel. His eyes were closed. He didn't make a sound.

Nessa felt cold all over. She didn't know what to do. Looking down, she saw a sudden gush of blood soak the mattress.

"Dear God, no," said Mrs. Lockett, shoving the baby into Nessa's arms. "Laura, start ripping up that sheet there, for rags. We gotta stop the bleeding."

Mrs. Lockett's voice sounded like noise in Nessa's ears. Things weren't happening nicely like they did for Mrs. Bell. Was Fanny Jo dying? And this baby, why wasn't it moving? She took it in the kitchen. Minnie got up to look, gently touching the blue cheeks. It had a head of dark, wet hair.

Nessa couldn't hold back her tears.

"Wait," said Rolly. He took the infant and laid it on the table, rubbing its small chest with his finger. "Maybe we can help him. Minnie, rub his arms. Nessa, take the bread off the warming rack and get me another towel."

"What're you doing?" asked Nessa.

"Last year I saw Mr. Button do this with one of his puppies after it was born not breathing. Rub, Minnie."

Rolly caressed the baby's throat with his thumb. "Come on, little fella," he said. "Come on." When it didn't respond, he picked it up by its tiny feet — holding it upside down — then slapped its back, not hard, but Nessa was shocked.

"Rolly!" she cried. "Why —"

A sound, like the weak mewing of a kitten, came from the baby. Liquid had oozed out of its mouth and nostrils, and the blue tone of its skin was beginning to turn grayish pink.

"Is he alive?" asked Minnie.

Nessa gently took him from Rolly, then wrapped him in the clean towel. "I think so," she said, "but he's so cold." She cradled him in her arm and leaned her face close to his. "He's barely breathing. Little boy, please open your eyes."

"Here," said Rolly. He came from the pantry with a cracker box and dumped the contents on the table. Lining it with a dish towel, he took the baby from Nessa and tucked him inside the makeshift bed. "This is what Mr. Button did with that last litter of puppies. Four were born dead, but he got the fifth one to start breathing."

Rolly went to the stove and touched the warming rack to feel the temperature. The box fit perfectly on top of the back of the range. This shelf was where Mrs. Lockett kept the plates and bread warm before serving a meal.

"Just right," he said. "Anyhow, after the pup warmed up for several hours, it was just fine. Spanky's a good ol' dog now."

"But, Rolly," said his sister, "this is a real baby, not a puppy."

"Yes, but Fanny Jo's too sick to take care of it right now and if he doesn't get warm —"

"Will he die?" Minnie's eyes filled with tears.

Rolly stroked her unbrushed hair, then glanced at Nessa. He didn't answer.

CHAPTER SEVENTEEN

Neighbors

Throughout the morning, Nessa and Rolly guarded the warming rack, making sure the temperature stayed even. Each time they got up, Green followed them, observing their every move.

Hour by hour, the baby's skin began to turn a healthier pink. His hair had dried into a soft brown fluff. When they noticed that his lips were moving, they put the box on the table and again massaged his arms and chest.

"You're doing good, little fella," said Rolly. "I wish the doc would get here and have a look at you."

Nessa stroked his cheek. "You're so handsome," she said, touching the tiny mouth with her finger. Immediately, he began sucking.

"Look!" Her voice was excited. "I think he's thirsty." She dipped her finger in water, then let the drips moisten his tongue. He swallowed again and again, soon falling asleep. They returned the box to the back of the stove.

"Mother," said Rolly, peeking into the parlor. "I think the baby's going to be all right."

Mrs. Lockett gave a tired smile. "Thank the Lord,"

she said. She leaned over Fanny Jo and whispered to her.
The young woman was pale and appeared to be sleeping.
Wads of bloody cloths were on the hearth, which Laura
was putting into the flames.

Just before noon, sleigh bells announced visitors.

Mrs. Bell, the blacksmith's wife, drove her sleigh up to
the back porch. Sitting beside her was Mrs. Applewood
with a basket on her lap. As Rolly ran out to stable the
horses, Nessa put coffee in the pot, filled it with water,
then set it on the stove. The bacon she had cooked earlier was on a platter ready to serve with eggs and potatoes
if anyone was hungry.

"The doctor hasn't come back from Fort Dodge yet,"
said Mrs. Bell as she unwrapped her cloak from her large
frame. Her brown hair was piled on top of her head. She
hugged Minnie against her cold skirt and smiled at Nessa.
"Hello, honey girls. Me and Mrs. Applewood came soon
as Hoss told us. Had to take Oliver to my neighbor's
first."

"Fanny Jo's real sick," said Minnie.

"My word. Where is she?"

Minnie led the women into the parlor where Fanny Jo
lay sleeping by the fire. After whispering with Mrs. Lockett they returned with her to the kitchen.

"We'll just keep praying that the worst is over," said
Mrs. Bell. "Poor thing. She needs lots of rest and all your
good care, Vivian. Now where's that little one?"

Nessa took the wooden box from the warming rack
and set it on the table.

"Well, I'll be." Mrs. Bell lifted the baby up for a good look. But at her touch, he wrinkled his face and let out a soft cry.

"Mrs. Bell," said Minnie, "your hands are still cold."

"My goodness, darlin', you're right." She covered the infant with the warm dish towel and lay him on the table. Opening the blanket partway so he wouldn't get chilled, she rotated the small hands and feet, straightened the knees, touched the abdomen, felt his neck. "Well, well," she said. "Vivian, thanks to the fast thinking of your family here, Fanny Jo's child might yet live."

Mrs. Applewood opened her basket and took out an assortment of clean rags, diaper pins, small woolen smocks, and a knit blanket. "For the new mother," she said. Her voice was soft. Nessa noticed that her face seemed gentler because her hair was brushed into a looser bun and there were wisps along her cheeks. Mrs. Applewood unfolded the blanket, holding it up to the light. The blue and brown yarn had been woven together in delicate rows.

"Made this myself some time ago," she said.

Mrs. Lockett fingered the wool. "Why it's just beautiful, Lillith. And soft."

Nessa was so accustomed to Mrs. Applewood's harshness, she was surprised to see her on this goodwill visit, and wondered why she had baby things to give away. As the room grew quiet, Nessa noticed the woman's eyes were moist.

"Would you like some coffee, Mrs. Applewood?" she asked, wanting to do something nice for her.

"That would be lovely."

Nessa brought out cups and saucers, then began setting the table for breakfast. Despite her fatigue, a sudden cheerfulness settled over her. The possibility that Fanny Jo and her baby might survive had lifted a heavy burden from her heart. And Mrs. Applewood being gentle was like the sun coming out on a cloudy day.

But something else touched her more than anything. When Mrs. Bell had spoken about Mrs. Lockett's family, she had included Nessa.

CHAPTER EIGHTEEN

———⟫◆⟪———

Snow Business

Two days after Christmas, Nessa and Minnie rode to school in Rolly's sled. Fresh snow had fallen in the night, and the prairie spread before them like a downy white quilt. The sun was rising into a blue sky. As Buttercup pranced along the unbroken path, the bells around her neck jingled through the crisp air.

"What are our lessons today?" Minnie asked when they pulled up to the schoolhouse. Nessa stepped down into four inches of snow, then reached up for Minnie. She held her by the waist so the girl could jump from the seat without becoming tangled in her skirt.

"Well," said Nessa, "first there's multiplication, then we'll memorize two proverbs. A spelling bee before lunch, then, afterward, penmanship. Also, there're some stories we'll take turns reading from Mr. Button's newspaper. Why do you ask?"

Minnie opened her lunch pail and took out a small carrot. Stroking Buttercup's neck, she held the carrot below his soft nose. There was loud crunching from the horse's jaw. "Well, it's so pretty outside," she answered. "I wish we could play hooky."

Nessa laughed. "But, Minnie, Mr. Applewood won't let me teach anymore if I keep finding reasons to cancel class. Come on, you can help me sweep snow off the steps while Rolly goes to town for Ivy and little Poppy."

Secretly, Nessa agreed it would be fun to close school for the day. Knowing Mary Ellen might come to class, however, made her cautious.

"Four times twenty-eight," Nessa read from her notes. She waited while the students wrote their answers on the blank newsprint supplied by Mr. Button. "Nineteen times six . . . twelve times seven." She noticed Mary Ellen was drawing circles across her paper, not numbers.

Nessa decided to ignore the doodling. She gazed out the window at the glistening snow. A pair of black-tailed jackrabbits bounded across the path, leaving a zigzag of prints as they headed for the creek. Nessa watched them chase each other, then faced her class. Suddenly, she didn't care if Mary Ellen criticized her.

"Does anyone here know how to make snowballs?" she asked. She smiled to herself, remembering the fabulous snowball fight she and Albert had last winter in the backyard of the orphanage. They had sneaked outside during a blizzard, when all the other children had been in the classroom doing lessons. Mr. Carey's punishment of no-supper-and-early-to-bed had been worth their fun.

Surprised faces looked up at Nessa. The new boy, Sven, raised his hand, then so did Lucy and Augusta. Big

Howard stood up. "There's a shovel in the barn, Miss Nessa. We can build a fort and have teams."

"Well, then," said Nessa, "I think it's time we got down to snow business. Hats and mittens first, please."

The clamor of children grabbing coats and running for the door delighted Nessa. Minnie was right. It was too nice to be stuck inside all day. She wasn't going to worry about the wolf, either, since Rolly had managed to shoot its paw.

Before the sun was overhead, there were two forts facing each other, each tall enough to hide crouching children. Arsenals of snowballs were piled inside the walls. Nessa stood by the barn so her students wouldn't think she was taking sides.

"One . . . two . . . three!" she shouted, and the battle began. Soon tiny craters dotted the field. Green raced back and forth, trying to bite the snowballs midair, then barking when they dissolved at her feet. For twenty minutes, the excited shrieks of children pierced the cold morning air. Even Mary Ellen joined in, the blur of her red cloak flashing up and down behind the wall. When the weapons had been used up, each team charged the other's fortress, trampling what remained.

Next, Ivy suggested a game of tag, which resulted in the students running circles around the barn and schoolhouse. Her thick, wool scarf protected her neck and ears from the wind as she yelled with laughter. Nessa joined them in races to the creek and back, stepping high and wide through the fresh drifts. She was relieved to see her friend with such energy and once again able to run out-doors.

Out of breath, Nessa stopped to rest along the river, near a grove of timber that had survived last summer's wildfire. She noticed that Big Howard and Rolly had climbed one of the trees. They sat quietly, straddling a branch and glancing toward the schoolhouse, apparently hoping no one had seen them. Nessa knew they were up to something. Finally, the girls returned to the riverbank.

"Yoo-hoo!" called Mary Ellen. "Rolly? Howard?" As she and the others looked among the brush, the red of her cloak stood out like the breast of a robin. Back and forth they tromped along the stream. Several minutes later, she called out again. Not thinking to look directly overhead, Mary Ellen planted her hands on her hips.

"Where in tarnation are you two?" In response, the boys bounced up and down on the limb. Clumps of snow showered down on the girls, followed by screams of sur-prise and threats. By the time the boys slid down the trunk and began their run for safety, they were covered with blasted snowballs, the girls in pursuit.

Nessa returned to the schoolhouse, where she watched from the step. Sometimes she wished she wasn't the teacher so she could climb a tree or chase a boy. "Time to eat!" she called to her students. "It's already afternoon."

As Nessa stood near the stove warming her hands, Mary Ellen came up to her. Leaning close enough to whisper, the girl said, "I bet you told the boys to do that, you wretched thing. If the school committee finds out that you would rather play than teach, they'll send you back to where you came from. Everyone's already talking about what a fool you are not to marry the preacher."

Nessa felt so refreshed from being outdoors and having observed her students having fun, she wasn't ruffled by the comment. "Mary Ellen," she said, looking the girl in the eye, "I'll take my chances with the school committee. And guess what else? Folks can say whatever they want about me getting married, but the decision is mine."

When Nessa and Minnie came in from the back porch with Rolly, the table was set for supper and Mrs. Lockett was at the stove.

"Wonderful news," she said. "Papa sent a letter. It's here in my pocket, honey."

"Oh!" cried Minnie, reaching into her mother's apron. "Read it for us, won't you, Nessa?"

Nessa sat beneath the lantern that hung from a rafter, unfolded the stationery, and began reading.

My dearest family,

As you can see, I am writing this by my own hand. At long last I have the use of my arm, and also have been learning to walk again. Five soldiers in my ward are returning to their homes this month. I pray I will be next on the discharge list. A drummer boy in the bed beside mine is an orphan with no family to welcome him, so I shall invite the lad to come with me to Prairie River. It is your generous

heart, Vivian, that allows me to do such a thing. With profound affection to Rolly and Minnie. How I miss you all,
Your loving Papa

When Nessa finished reading, she looked up. Mrs. Lockett was smiling at her children. Nessa wasn't surprised at what Mrs. Lockett said next.

"Well, my darlin's, it looks like your father is bringing us another new member of the family. We'll need to make some space and put more food on the table, but I know our good Lord will provide."

CHAPTER NINETEEN

Little Kit

Wind wore away the snow, exposing tufts of buffalo grass along the trail. Inside the house, rugs rolled up against the doors stopped the drafts, but cold air still seeped in around the windows.

When the baby was five days old, Fanny Jo sat up on her cot. It was New Year's Eve. Her braid hung over her shoulder, her cheeks were gaunt. The only energy she'd had was to nurse her son. "Mrs. Lockett," she said in a hoarse voice. "May I have a bath, please?"

"Why, of course, my dear. We'll get the water warmin' right away."

Laura helped Nessa take the tub down from its peg on the wall and set it in front of the stove, the warmest place in the house. On a chair next to it they put clean towels and a bar of lavender soap, then filled the kettle from the water bucket by the back door. From hooks in the low ceiling, they hung two blankets, which made a cozy room within the kitchen.

They leaned down to peek at the baby in its cracker box. He was wrapped securely, sleeping on his side.

Nessa touched his downy hair and wanted to say his name, but didn't know what it was.

Maybe now that Fanny Jo was feeling better, she would name her son.

Nessa opened the back door to Rolly's knocking. He came into the kitchen carrying a small wooden cradle.

"What's that you have there?" asked Fanny Jo. She was in the rocking chair, her long brown hair drying before the stove. Her son lay on her lap.

"I was at the Applewoods'," he said. "The missus brought this out, said she wanted you to have it."

"My goodness, that's kind of her," said Fanny Jo. For a moment she was thoughtful, then she smiled at Rolly. "Minnie tells me you picked out a name."

He set the cradle on the floor. "Well . . ." he hesitated. "It's just someone I met once. He was brave and fought hard to stay alive."

"Who is it, dear?"

"Kit Carson," he answered. "Remember when he came here before Thanksgiving, he was helping with the Indian Treaties?"

"I do remember. Laura and I saw him eating in the officers' mess hall."

"Anyhow," said Rolly, "I like his courage and that he tries to do good."

Fanny Jo looked down at her son. "Kit?" she said. His face turned toward her voice. "Kit Carson Holmes. What a fine name. Thank you, Rolly. I'll write to my husband this evening. I'm certain he would approve, and that as soon as he gets leave, he'll come visit."

Nessa and Laura hurried along the trail to town, to mail Fanny Jo's letter, Green leading the way. The skies were clear, no clouds. Nessa couldn't wait for Wildwing to be big enough for her to ride, so she could get back and forth faster. Only in winter had she become nervous about being on the prairie. Sudden blizzards were one thing and Indians another, but wolves worried her the most.

At Mr. Filmore's store, Laura gave the letter to the clerk and paid fifty cents for its delivery to Fort Dodge, a two-day ride southwest. He told her the next stage heading that way might be tomorrow or another week, depending on the weather. The girls stood by the potbellied stove, warming themselves.

In the store, Ivy greeted them each with an oatmeal cookie she had just baked and a steaming cup of cocoa. Laughing at Green's begging paw, Ivy kneeled beside the dog.

"All right, girl," she said. "Here's one for you, too."

Nessa was thankful to see her friend so cheerful, that she hadn't become ill from the Christmas dance or from playing in the snow the other day. She wanted to discuss the soldier with Ivy, but they hadn't been alone yet. And at school she didn't want to risk the little ones overhearing their conversation.

"Papa's at the hospital visiting those soldiers," Ivy said. She scratched away ice on the window, then pointed outside. Across from the parade ground was a low sod building with smoke rising from its chimney.

"They've been feverish," continued Ivy, "and this morning when the doctor came by, he said the one bitten in the neck started having convulsions."

"Oh, dear," said Laura. She set her cup on the counter and began buttoning her coat. "I hope it's not rabies. Nessa, come with me, please? I want them to know they saved Fanny Jo's life and mine." Laura bolted out the door, wrapping her scarf around her neck.

CHAPTER TWENTY

————◆◆◆————

The Hospital

In the narrow entryway of the hospital, Laura and Nessa shook the snow from their hems and unwrapped their scarves to hang on the coat hooks. A door to their left was the apothecary with shelves of jars and bottles. To their right was the ward. They leaned into that doorway, looking for the two soldiers.

Nessa was surprised to see how spacious and clean the room was. Beds were not the narrow cots she had imagined, but were wide with thick mattresses. Windows allowed in sunlight, and the whitewashed walls gave a cheery appearance. An iron stove in the center radiated heat.

"There they are," Laura whispered. "Those two over there." She nodded toward a corner where a man lay with a splinted leg. Next to him in another bed was a man with a bandage around his neck. A rope at his waist held him to the mattress. Mr. Filmore sat on a chair between them, reading aloud from a Bible.

Upon noticing the girls, the doctor hurried over to the doorway. "I'm sorry, misses. It's better if you don't see them like this. The fellow with the leg wound has had a high fever for two days."

The girls glanced across the room.

Then the doctor pointed to the other man. "Things are worse for him, bit in the neck. Since early this morning he's been in and out of delirium."

After a moment, Laura said, "Is it rabies?"

"I'm afraid so, young lady." He lifted her cloak from its hook, handing it to her, then did the same with Nessa's. Motioning for them to leave the hospital he said, "I'm sorry there isn't better news, but —"

A scream pierced the air. Chills ran up Nessa's spine when she realized it came from one of the beds.

"Excuse me," he said, hastening back inside, closing the door behind him. But the door swung open on its hinge as his sleeve caught on the knob. Nessa stared in horror at the scene before her.

One of the men who had been bitten by the wolf was staring at the floor, shrieking like a wild animal. He tried to claw his way out of bed, but two soldiers and Mr. Filmore wrestled him onto the mattress. As the man's body jumped with convulsions, the others held him down so he couldn't hurt himself.

Nessa was so frightened, she couldn't swallow. She'd never seen anything like this. She'd never heard such a panicked cry. Only when she felt Laura pulling her arm was she able to turn away.

The girls were distraught as they put on their coats and rushed outside where Green had been waiting for them.

She loped beside them as they found the path to the boardinghouse. Dark clouds were building in the sky, and the air temperature had dropped far below freezing. Wind tugged at their skirts. They wrapped their scarves around their necks high enough to cover their cheeks. Laura's tears froze on her eyelashes.

"I wish I knew how to pray," she sobbed. "My words . . . they seem too small to reach the ear of God."

Nessa looked at Laura. Sometimes she, too, wondered if her prayers were strong enough for God to hear. But as she pictured the dying soldiers, her heart so ached for them, her words came naturally. She took Laura's mittened hand in hers.

"Dear Jesus," she said, her voice being swept away by the wind, *"please console those brave men. Even though they're suffering, we pray they'll feel Your presence and that they'll be with You in Heaven. Amen."*

Above the edge of her scarf, Laura's red cheeks lifted with a smile. "Nessa, I'm glad you and I are becoming friends after all."

CHAPTER TWENTY-ONE

New Boarders

$\mathcal{M}$rs. Lockett was frosting a cake as the girls came in the kitchen door, snowflakes in their hair and on their sleeves. Nessa was still upset about what they'd seen at the hospital, but she didn't think she could talk about it without crying. Maybe this evening she and Laura could tell the others.

"I was about to send Rolly after you two," said Mrs. Lockett. "When I went to the henhouse ten minutes ago, I could smell snow in the air. Knew a storm was comin'."

Fanny Jo was on a stool, peeling potatoes. Color had returned to her cheeks and today her hair was swept up in ivory combs. She smiled at Minnie, who sat in the rocker, carefully holding the baby in her arms. Her braids were tied at the ends with blue ribbons, which matched her smock. Mr. Button's rag doll was beside Minnie, also dressed in blue.

"Tell them, Mama," she said.

Relieved by this distraction, Nessa said, "Tell us what?"

Mrs. Lockett handed the frosting spoon to Rolly for

him to lick, then wiped her hands on her apron. "Well," she began, "we have a nice surprise for everyone."

All eyes turned to her. "I've invited the sisters to stay here with us. They can have the upstairs guest room. It'll give Fanny Jo a chance to get back to her old self, and we can all help with the baby."

Mrs. Lockett began grating a chunk of dark chocolate to sprinkle on the icing. "Not many boarders come through in the winter, anyhow, and I'll be awful glad for the company. Last January it was just me, Minnie, Rolly, and an occasional travelin' man. Now I'll have all of you under my roof. It'll make our dark days go faster, don't you think? That is, if you're up to it, Laura?"

Laura's face broke into a smile. "Oh, I'm so glad. I love it here, it's much warmer than our cabin and not as lonesome. And, Mrs. Lockett, we'll pay for our keep. I have my job with the baker, plus money saved."

The woman waved her hand as if shooing a fly. "Nonsense. I won't take your money. Besides, bakers get up too early — I don't want you havin' to walk into town at three o'clock in the mornin'. Too dangerous this time of year. The Lord will provide, He always has. I still thank Him for that stranger who paid my bill at Applewoods' — such a wonderful surprise that was. What I'm sayin' is, that will help see us through."

Nessa turned away, not wanting Mrs. Lockett to see her face. She didn't want her expression to reveal that it had been she — Nessa — who secretly paid the debt. She bent down to look at the cake.

"Is this for our birthday girl?" she asked.

"Yes, indeed," said Mrs. Lockett. "At nine o'clock tonight she'll be seven years old, won't you, honey?" She beamed at her daughter who was taking her job seriously, caring for the baby. Though Minnie's legs were too short to touch the ground, she swung them just enough to make the chair rock.

Suddenly, a shudder shook the house. Wind gusted under the doors and moaned through the eaves. Rolly hurried to roll up the smaller rugs to press against the drafts. "Lucky I brought in all that wood and chips," he said. "And, Nessa, you and Laura got here just in time. Watch, in a minute we won't even be able to see the barn."

Nessa stood at the window. How she loved a storm when she was safe inside, and knowing Wildwing and the other animals were in the barn, also safe. Far across the prairie, a white curtain dropped from the sky and began moving toward them. She could see through it, to dark clouds on the other side. The storm appeared to have wisps of gauze spreading before it.

"Snow, sure enough," Rolly said. "See how fast it's blowing this way?"

A pounding on the front door interrupted them. Startled, everyone looked up.

"Son," said Mrs. Lockett, "quickly now. Whoever it is, invite them in to warm up."

From the parlor came the noise of the door opening, then a familiar voice. Nessa's heart sunk. Not now. Someone she didn't feel like seeing today.

Mary Ellen came into the kitchen. Her red cloak and

hood were covered with snow. Green met her with a wagging tail and nudged her mitten for a pet.

"Good heavens, child." Mrs. Lockett rushed forward to take her things and usher her before the stove. "What're you doin' out in this weather? Does your mother know where you are?"

"Yes, ma'am. She made this taffy." Mary Ellen handed her a parcel wrapped in calico. "We heard it was Minnie's birthday. Also, there's something here for Nessa. Hello, Nessa."

"Hello, Mary Ellen."

Mrs. Lockett draped the red cloak over a chair to dry. "Well, dear, on account of this storm you must stay the night with us. I just pray your parents won't worry."

"Oh, they don't worry when I'm with Bonnie Prince Charlie."

"Bonnie Prince Charlie?"

"My horse."

Rolly ran to the parlor and cupped his hands against the window to look out. "He's standing in the wind, Ma. I'll go put him in the barn right away. Mary Ellen, you never should've left home with storm clouds rising. Didn't you look outside first?"

With a loud sigh, Mary Ellen turned her gaze to the ceiling. "We rode fast," she said. "Besides, I wasn't planning to be here all the live-long day. In Ohio, we never had such miserable tempests because at least we had *trees* everywhere to slow down the wind." She sighed again.

"Go ahead, son," said Mrs. Lockett, ignoring Mary

Ellen's complaint. She opened the parcel and took out the taffy, which was wrapped in waxed paper. Next, Mrs. Lockett held up a doll about ten inches tall. Its head was porcelain, painted with blue eyes and a red mouth. It was dressed in a hoopskirt with tiny high-buttoned shoes.

"How lovely," she said.

"That's for Minnie," said Mary Ellen. "It was mine, but I don't want it anymore. The hair's not real."

The kitchen was quiet until the birthday girl remembered her manners. "Thank you, Mary Ellen. She's awful pretty."

At this, Nessa busied herself setting the table with plates and spoons, then bowls for soup. She wasn't eager to see what Red Riding Hood had brought her.

From the fold of the cloth, Mrs. Lockett pulled out a small wooden box. It was tied with string. "And this?" she asked.

"Oh, that's for Nessa, from our pastor. He showed us what's inside and I tell you, it's very grown-up. Only someone with poor judgment wouldn't appreciate it."

CHAPTER TWENTY-TWO

The Temptation

Nessa held the box. Everyone in the kitchen was watching her. She felt frustrated that Mary Ellen Whipple had intruded on their peaceful afternoon, and more so that she was spending the night. The way storms on the prairie lasted, who knew how long they'd be stuck with her?

"Open it," said Mary Ellen.

Indecision seized Nessa. She was curious about the contents, but did not want a bossy girl telling her what to do. Whatever was inside the box, Nessa probably would be the only one not to *ooh* and *aah* over it, because she did not want anything from Reverend McDuff in the first place.

Why a gift? It wasn't Christmas or her birthday.

Suddenly, she realized she could return this just as she had his letter months earlier. Feeling a growing sense of purpose, Nessa put the box in Mary Ellen's hand.

"Please give this back to the preacher."

"You ornery little thing," the girl said. "Are you mad?

Don't you want to know what it is? Well, I'll tell you what —"

"That's enough, Mary Ellen." Mrs. Lockett took the box from her, walked into the pantry, and set it on the top shelf. "When the storm's over, you may ride Bonnie Prince Charlie home and return this to the reverend. Tonight, we'll make up a bed for you in front of the fire — but in the meantime, let's have some supper. It's Minnie's birthday."

Nessa lay under her buffalo robe, staring at the bare white window. The wind pushed and pulled against the glass, swishing snow against its surface. She wondered why Mary Ellen was so snappish. After supper, Nessa had tried to be friendly by inviting her to play the reading game, in which several people sit in a circle and take turns reading from a book. The last person isn't allowed to read, but must instead make up an ending.

"No, thank you," Mary Ellen had said about joining them. "That's rather childish if you ask me."

This rebuke had troubled Nessa, but her thoughts now turned to Reverend McDuff's gift. What was it? Mary Ellen's vague description taunted her. The longer she lay there, the more awake she became.

At last, she slipped out of bed, covered her shoulders with her shawl, and went downstairs. The floor was cold under her bare feet. She wished Green wasn't following her, but to whisper a command would make too much noise.

When Nessa passed the parlor, she could see the sleeping form of Mary Ellen in front of the hearth. She paused to make sure her steps hadn't aroused her, then went into the pantry.

Reaching up to the top shelf, she felt in the dark for the box. She took it down, careful not to knock anything over, crept upstairs, and closed her door.

She sat on her bed. By the light of her candle, she untied the string and took off the lid. She gasped at what lay inside.

It was the most beautiful thing Nessa had ever seen. A watch on a dainty silver chain.

A note lay beneath it. Unfolding it, she held it close to her candle to read.

Nessa dear,
    Please accept this gift, from someone who has known you since you were four years old. Of course, you knew my sister and that she passed away in childbed. She, too, knew you when you were a little girl and would certainly be pleased for you to have this.
Yours sincerely,
Reverend M. J. McDuff

Nessa got under her robe to warm up, then read the letter three more times. How she would love to have such a pretty piece of jewelry, and something so useful, too. She remembered his sister from church. Lizzie McDuff had always slipped a piece of candy into Nessa's hand, then Albert's, when they fidgeted during the last hymn. How they adored her! This watch had hung from her graceful neck where she would click open the lid to show them the time. *Not too much longer,* she would whisper.

The memory of this touched Nessa anew. *Lord, now what?* If only the man offering this gift were an uncle or even Mr. Button, not someone who wanted to marry her. She closed her eyes. Some minutes passed before she realized she'd fallen asleep.

Quickly, she returned the note and watch to its box, then tiptoed downstairs. When she emerged from the pantry, she heard the rustle of someone moving in the parlor.

In the glow of the firelight, Nessa could see that Mary Ellen was sitting up on her bed, watching her.

CHAPTER TWENTY-THREE

Snowed In

The next morning it was still snowing with a fierce wind. Rolly had gotten up early to feed the animals, using the long rope tied between the house and barn to find his way through the blowing snow. Before supper, Laura and Nessa would take their turns with the rope and do the chores together.

There were seven people at breakfast. An oil lamp hanging from the wall cast a warm glow over the group as the baby slept in his cradle by the stove. Nessa helped Mrs. Lockett fill everyone's bowl with oatmeal, then she passed around a platter of baked cinnamon apples. When she got to Mary Ellen, the girl said, "Thank you," but would not look Nessa in the eye.

She wondered if Mary Ellen was going to tell everyone about their encounter in the middle of the night or keep the matter to herself. Now Nessa was embarrassed to have made such a dramatic gesture yesterday, refusing Reverend McDuff's gift. If others knew she had secretly opened it after all, it might appear that she had changed her mind about the marriage proposal.

There was something else. Nessa couldn't stop thinking about the beautiful watch. She wanted to keep it. How elegant it would look against her scarlet dress, especially while standing in front of her students. It was similar to the one that Miss Eva had worn.

Rolly was sitting across the table from Mary Ellen. "Please pass the cream," he said to her. As she handed him the small pitcher he said, "Your horse sure is handsome, Mary Ellen. I reckon you can ride him pretty far and fast if you've a mind to."

The girl appeared to be thinking as she spread molasses onto her bread. "I would," she answered, "except my parents are afraid I'll get lost on the prairie or that Indians will kidnap me like that girl living with the Cheyenne. I'm supposed to stay in sight of the fort." She dipped her bread into her cocoa, then took a bite. She was careful to wipe her mouth with a napkin.

"Actually," she said, placing her napkin in her lap, "Mama's probably worried sick right now. I've never spent a night away from home."

Mrs. Lockett reached into the cradle to pick up the baby, who had begun to fuss. She held him against her shoulder, patting his back. "Honey," she said to Mary Ellen, "soon as the skies clear, Rolly'll escort you home. Meanwhile, there's nothin' any of us can do except stay warm and enjoy one another's company."

The storm lasted all day and the next night. Nessa was relieved that no one had mentioned the gift — so far.

The following morning after she had dressed, Rolly came to her room.

"Isn't it beautiful?" he said, pointing to her window. Blue sky reached to the horizon and the sun was shining. Snow came up to her sill. "It's just a big ol' drift from the wind," he said, "but we'll have to climb out here to get to the barn. Can't open the kitchen door yet or even the one in front. Porches are waist-deep in snow. Yippee." He turned and ran downstairs, making the noise of three boys.

Nessa loved his enthusiasm. She also loved knowing Mary Ellen would go home as soon as a path was cleared to the barn. When she went downstairs, the girl had folded her blankets and stacked them by the hearth. She was sitting with Minnie by a sunny window, a *Harper's Magazine* opened across their laps.

"Read, won't you please?" asked the seven-year-old.

"Keep going, Minnie, you're doing quite well."

Nessa observed the two. The few times Mary Ellen had come to class, she didn't stay long enough to do any lessons, but would leave before it was her turn to read aloud. And the last two nights, she had refused to play the reading game.

Does Mary Ellen even know how to read? she wondered.

As Nessa set out cups and saucers for their morning tea, her frustration with the girl softened into curiosity. She prayed silently, glancing over at the chair. *Here I am again, Jesus, asking You to help me be kind to Mary Ellen. Please show me how to be her friend.*

After breakfast, Rolly ran upstairs, threw open Nessa's window, then slid down the frozen bank, yelling, "Yay-yippee-yay!"

"Wait here," he called up to her after recovering his feet. "Soon as I bring out Bonnie Prince Charlie, get Mary Ellen. If she's scared, just tell her it's fun!"

Mary Ellen stood by Nessa's bed, wrapped in her red cloak and hood. She put on her mittens, then tucked the rejected gift inside a pocket. As she put one foot out the window, she steadied herself against the casing, then brought up her other foot so she was sitting on the sill, her skirt blanketing her knees and ankles.

Turning around to Nessa, she said, "Reverend McDuff's going to be awful sad when I give this back to him. Maybe Mama and Papa were right, that you're not smart enough to know what's good for you. And to think you're the teacher — how droll!"

"Is that so?" said Nessa. Without waiting for a reply, she put her hand on Mary Ellen's back and gave her a good shove. The girl's legs and petticoats flew up over her head as she slid down to Rolly and the waiting horses. Her shriek of surprise was lost in the wind.

Nessa slammed the window shut. When she realized Mrs. Lockett was in the hallway holding the stack of blankets, she was ashamed for having pushed Mary Ellen.

"Well, my dear," said Mrs. Lockett with a slight smile, "there are better ways to bid farewell to our guests. I reckon your method will keep folks talkin' and speculatin' all through the winter."

CHAPTER TWENTY-FOUR

———◆———

The Making of a Pearl

$\mathcal{M}$oments later, Nessa joined Mrs. Lockett in her room. The window looked out over the creek where a small herd of buffalo was breaking a path for water. Their shaggy coats had icicles hanging from their necks and bellies.

"That girl makes me so mad," said Nessa. She had confessed to Mrs. Lockett about the beautiful watch and how Mary Ellen had seen her return it to the pantry. "Now she'll tell her mother and probably Reverend McDuff, then the whole town will know. Every time I decide to be nice to Mary Ellen, she says something that makes me want to slap her."

"I know, dear."

"But why? I try to be pleasant, and I've been praying, waiting for God to do something." Nessa sighed, her breath fogging the windowpane. After a moment, the glass again was clear. "It sure felt good to push her out the window, though."

"I reckon it did, darlin'. But consider this before you do it again. God often puts people in our life to test us and help us grow. Will you be kind to Mary Ellen only if she's nice to you? Can you show respect to our pastor even though you don't see eye to eye?"

Nessa watched the buffalo make their slow way along the frozen banks. Birds flew up from the bare tree limbs at their approach. "It's hard," she finally answered. "Sometimes I just don't feel like trying."

The woman took out her basket of knitting. When a ball of blue yarn tumbled out and rolled into the hall, Green raced to retrieve it. She carried it in her mouth to Mrs. Lockett, but would not let go.

"Drop it," said Nessa.

Green wagged her tail.

"Drop it right now."

Green looked at the ceiling, then the wall, as if thinking about other things. Finally, she released the yarn, now soggy.

"What a funny dog you are," said Mrs. Lockett, patting the fuzzy ears. "Thank you, Green. Nessa honey, back to what we were sayin', about the folks who upset you . . . the way I see it, our good Lord is just makin' you into a pearl. Same way that He puts folks in our life to bother us, God puts a grain of sand into the oyster. Somethin' happens inside the shell with the sand irritatin' the soft parts. After time, a precious jewel is born, the pearl. I don't know how it happens, but it does."

Because snowdrifts had covered the windows, making the downstairs dark, Mrs. Lockett sat upstairs to catch the sunlight, her knitting needles clicking like a clock. She smiled at Nessa. "I'm gonna teach you how to knit, honey.

Makin' somethin' with your hands frees up the mind to think and pray. Plus you have somethin' useful when you finish."

A rapping at Nessa's window echoed into the hallway.

Nessa hurried to her room. Peering in from the tall snowbank was Ivy, waving two letters. A scarf was wrapped around her head and neck, her cheeks were red from the cold. Nessa could see Rolly down below, leading Butter-cup to the barn.

As Ivy climbed in the window, she hugged her friend. "Don't worry, Nessa, I rode with Rolly. He saw me on the trail and pulled me up into his saddle. I'm plenty warm, and Papa knows where I am. Here, these letters came a few days ago, before the storm. I'm dying to know who wrote you. Oh, remember the soldier from the dance? He came to see me after breakfast this morning!"

Nessa sat on her bed. Pulling her buffalo robe onto both of them for warmth, she stared at the letters in her hand. Her heart leaped with excitement when she recog-nized Albert's wobbly handwriting. Now Ivy's voice seemed far away.

". . . so Papa poured him a cup of coffee and —"

"I'm sorry," said Nessa. She held up the letters. "I truly want to hear your news, Ivy, but —"

"Oh, dear, I've been carrying on. Please forgive me. Is one from Albert?"

Nessa smiled. "Yes . . . but this other one, I'm not sure." Ink from the postmark had smeared, but she could make out the word *Wisconsin*. With her fingernail she broke open the wax seal and pulled out a piece of stationery. The paper was so thin it crackled like the skin of an onion. Nessa scanned to the bottom.

"It's from my aunt Britta!" Her voice was excited, but she could feel the beginning of tears. Her aunt was alive.

"My dearest niece . . ."

Nessa began reading, but was overcome with emotion. She covered her face with her hands and wept. A blood relative had called her *dearest*.

Ivy put her arms around Nessa and hugged her. "Would you like me to read it for you?"

She nodded, handing Ivy the letter.

". . . How overjoyed your uncle Erik and I were to hear from you. Now that we have finally found one another, there is so much to tell you. Your brothers are standing next to me at the table, watching my pen and asking me to translate. They understand some English, but were raised speaking Danish. Per and Lief are nearly eleven years old and are beside themselves to hear they have a sister. They help with the dairy like grown men, you'd be so proud.

Oh, but where to begin, my dear? Let me first say, your parents loved you and never dreamed you would have been raised without family. The day after your papa's funeral, you were taken from us against our wishes, by a relative who thought he knew best. Such a tiny little girl you were, and how we grieved. After a long search, we thought we had lost you forever.

I am out of paper now, but will close with these words, dear Vanessa: Your grandparents yearn to see you while they still live, as do your cousins and, of course, I, your mother's own sister, your aunt Britta."

Ivy folded the stationery and returned it to its envelope. "Oh, Nessa," she said, "does this mean you'll leave Prairie River?"

Nessa's tears wouldn't stop. She couldn't raise her head to look at Ivy. The trunk beside her bed was full of memories and mystery, but this letter brought something new. At long last she had found her real family.

And they wanted her.

CHAPTER TWENTY-FIVE

A Long Way from Home

Per and Lief Clemens. My brothers. Nessa stood in front of her students, trying to concentrate on the sentences she was dictating, but her thoughts kept returning to the details of Aunt Britta's letter. *What do they look like and do they resemble our father? What do their voices sound like? Would I speak Danish, too, if someone hadn't taken me away?*

Oh, Lord, show me what to do, please! I want to know them and to be their big sister. Should I stay here or —

"Teacher?"

Nessa looked up from her book. "Yes, Augusta?"

The girl pointed to Poppy, who had laid her head down on her desk. Nessa walked over to the small girl to feel her forehead. It was hot and her scalp was damp with sweat. Nessa's throat tightened. She needed to get her home as soon as possible, but knew it would be dangerous to leave the other children alone.

It was with some relief that she regarded Mary Ellen's empty seat, because at this moment she didn't want to face another unpleasant exchange of words. It was bad

enough that the school committee seemed ready to crit-
icize Nessa's every move.

"Boys and girls," she said, making a decision as she
spoke. "Poppy's sick and needs her mother. We're going
to go together — all of us — to Officers' Row, then when
she's safe at home, we'll continue our lessons in the fort's
library. The colonel himself told me we could hold class
there anytime we need to."

Within minutes, Nessa was leading the warmly
dressed children to town. Rolly drove ahead with Poppy
in the back of his sled, protected from the wind with
blankets, Ivy beside her.

As they walked through the cold sunshine, Nessa prayed
for Poppy Sullivan and prayed that the wolf wouldn't
find them. Soon, though, her prayers blended into
thoughts about her faraway family.

And about Albert's letter.

It was tucked inside her sleeve where she could feel its
crisp paper. She wanted to take it out and read it again,
but did not want to be distracted, for she must hurry the
children along, watching for their safety. Green circled
the group, running back and forth as if they were a flock
of sheep.

"Good dog," Nessa called to her, "that's a good girl,
Green."

Nessa heard the jangling of harnesses and rumble of
hooves, and shaded her eyes against the glare of snow to
see better. In the distance, a unit of soldiers on horseback
was riding toward town with a covered wagon. It appeared

to be a delivery of some importance because several cav-
alrymen from the fort were galloping out to meet them.

Nessa worried about Poppy. From the library window,
she observed the doctor walking from the hospital toward
Officers' Row, which was a line of tents and sod buildings. The wind blew the tails of his coat behind him and
caught his hat just as his hand rescued it. When he went
into Lieutenant Sullivan's quarters, Nessa turned her attention back to her students.

It frustrated her that Mary Ellen Whipple didn't seem
to care about learning, for this was the third day this week
the girl wasn't in class. The others, however, were now
looking at Nessa with eagerness. Touched by their respect for her, she smiled at them and began dictation.

While the children practiced their penmanship, Nessa
took out Albert's letter. Now she understood why he
hadn't yet come to Prairie River. A horse had kicked his
editor in the ribs, and unable to work, the man had asked
Albert to take over the printing press until he recovered.
She again read his words:

"... but when I saw Reverend McDuff get on that
stage heading west, I felt like a wild horse tied up.
Nessa, please forgive me for not following him right
then like I promised. I've been praying for God to
give you courage, and I pray every single day that
you will not marry that man. HE DOES NOT
KNOW YOU. Fond Salutations, Albert, Tempo-
rary Assistant Editor, Missouri Daily Gazette."

Nessa looked up. Outside, some soldiers were leading an Indian girl to Officers' Row. She was in a buckskin dress with knee-high moccasins. A woman wearing a hoopskirt came out onto the wooden sidewalk, a shawl over her shoulders, to greet them. She opened her arms for the girl, then guided her into her house. Curious children who did not attend school ran to look in the windows.

Ivy came to the front of the class. "Nessa," she whispered, "that must be the girl who lived with Indians. Papa said the army was giving the tribe a dozen horses and all sorts of trinkets for her release. The poor thing's an orphan now and such a long way from home. I hope there're relatives back where she came from."

Nessa stood with Ivy at the window, looking out. She returned Albert's letter to her sleeve. "So do I," she said, thinking about her own family.

CHAPTER TWENTY-SIX

A Bit of Romance

The next morning, Nessa and Ivy were in Mr. Filmore's store, unpacking a crate of canned peaches and lining up the tins along a shelf.

"Papa," said Ivy, "when can we visit the girl who lived with Indians?"

"Soon enough, I reckon," he said. "Some officers' wives are getting clothes for her and no doubt will see to a bath. The trader said she's not saying much and seems sad. Maybe having you girls to talk with will lift her spirits."

Nessa and Ivy glanced at each other, but said nothing. They, too, knew what it was like to have lost their mothers and siblings.

The bell jingled against the door as a soldier stepped inside, bringing with him the smell of cold, fresh air. The buttons on his dark blue coat were polished and matched his brass belt buckle. His pants were light blue. At the sight of his uniform, Ivy's face brightened and she gave Nessa a small nudge.

"Good afternoon, Mr. Filmore," he said, taking off his cap. "Hello, Miss Ivy. How're you today?"

Ivy blushed. "Fine, thank you."

Mr. Filmore cleared his throat, regarding his daughter with a raised eyebrow.

"Oh, pardon my poor manners," said Ivy. "I'd like to introduce you to my friend. Her name is Nessa, and she's also our schoolteacher."

"How 'do, Miss Nessa. Name's Pennsylvania Lee, but folks call me Penn. You can, too."

"Hello," said Nessa. She wasn't ready to be so familiar with a soldier, especially now that she recognized him as the one who had almost kissed Ivy during the Christmas party.

After chatting a few minutes with Mr. Filmore, the soldier paid him two dollars for a tin of oysters and some peppermints. Smiling at the girls, he put on his cap and went out the door.

Ivy grabbed Nessa's arm to whisper in her ear. "Remember him from the barn dance?"

"So?"

"He comes in nearly every day," said Ivy. "I like him. He writes me poetry, but whatever you do, *please* don't tell Papa that."

Nessa looked at her friend. "You're too young to like a soldier."

"I'm fifteen now, and he's eighteen. That's exactly the ages my mother and father were when they got married."

"But . . ." Nessa didn't know what she wanted to say. Why did Ivy have to be thinking about romance, especially when she — Nessa — was fleeing from the idea of marriage?

Suddenly, she felt bottled up with worries. In addition to Reverend McDuff, there was the matter of Aunt Britta's letter. At last, Nessa had learned of her real family. Since they wanted her to return to them, shouldn't she? But how could she bring herself to leave the Locketts or Ivy? And what about her students? As their teacher, she had responsibilities.

Nessa's head hurt.

"I have to go now, Ivy," she said, putting on her coat and hurrying out the door.

The wind was cold. Nessa hunched her shoulders and buried her chin into her scarf. She felt like running home to lock herself in her room. If she hadn't promised Poppy a visit, she would do just that.

The plank sidewalk in front of Officers' Row had been shoveled, but blowing snow had coated it with ice. Nessa stepped carefully onto dry spots, the wind lifting the hem of her skirt with her long strides.

Smoke curled from Lieutenant Sullivan's chimney, and the roof was fringed with icicles. Nessa knocked on the door. Lace curtains framed one of the windows and allowed Nessa a glimpse into the cozy living quarters.

"Hello, dear, how good to see you," said Mrs. Sullivan when Nessa was let in by a Negro woman. "Come warm yourself. Edwina, won't you please bring Miss Nessa and me some cocoa with hot milk?"

The woman lowered her eyes, but managed a smile for the schoolteacher. "Yes'm," she said. "I be right there."

Poppy was asleep on a cot in front of the iron stove that heated the small room. There was a piano in a corner and dark green velvet chairs on either side of a window. Despite the fire, Nessa could feel a cold draft on her ankles. There was no rug on the earthen floor, nor a footstool where she could lift her feet off the ground.

"Please make yourself comfortable," Mrs. Sullivan said, motioning to the sofa. As soon as Nessa sat on the prickly velvet, a retriever bounded into the room, put its front paws on the cushions, and boosted itself up. It curled beside Nessa and laid its head across her lap with a sigh.

"Hello, Yellow Dog," Nessa said, petting the ears that were so familiar. Yellow Dog had been Peter's. After his funeral, the Sullivans had given one of her puppies to Nessa. That is how Green came to be hers.

"The surgeon told us Poppy is on the mend, but she must stay inside for at least a week. He promised to check on her twice a day." Mrs. Sullivan set down her cup with a delicate clatter. She glanced out the window where they could see the sod building of the hospital.

"But those two soldiers attacked by the wolf aren't as fortunate as my daughter." Her voice was soft. "Last night, I knelt right here and pleaded with Jesus to end their suffering, for my husband has been visiting them and described their terrible agonies. And do you know, Nessa, sometime in the night God answered my prayer. I know this only because when the surgeon came this morning he told me both soldiers had passed away in the wee hours."

Mrs. Sullivan offered Nessa a cookie from the plate brought in by Edwina. "If only the Lord would answer all our prayers so quickly, yes?"

Nessa looked at the kindness in the woman's face and wondered if she was remembering Peter's rattlesnake bite. "Yes, ma'am," she said. "I surely do wish so myself."

CHAPTER TWENTY-SEVEN

Crooked Stripes

The next week when Mary Ellen again missed school three days in a row, Nessa decided to visit the Whipples, to see if she was ill.

"I just wish Reverend McDuff wasn't living there, too," Nessa told Mrs. Lockett the following Saturday as they washed dishes together. "Even though Mary Ellen's older than I am, she's still a student and I should check on her, don't you think?"

Mrs. Lockett unfolded a clean dish towel and began drying a plate. "Good idea, dear. How 'bout takin' Rolly with you? On Buttercup you're up higher, better able to see what's around — that wolf ain't been tracked down yet — and it's faster if a storm happens to be comin'."

Nessa thought to herself that it would be good not to face the minister alone. She looked around the kitchen. Fanny Jo was in the rocker nursing her baby, her eyes closed as she hummed a lullaby. Laura sat at the table cracking walnuts for a spice cake. Minnie was at her side, stirring the nuts into a large bowl of batter. The aroma of spices and fresh coffee made Nessa want to stay here all afternoon. She didn't want to leave this warm place where she'd always been made to feel welcome.

Rolly pulled Nessa up into the saddle behind him. She sat astride with her skirt flowing out over her knees. Wool leggings covered her legs, and her shoes were buttoned high over wool socks. She wrapped her scarf around her neck and over her head, to protect her ears from the wind.

When they arrived at the Whipples' house, they led Buttercup into the barn so the horse would be out of the cold, then walked to the front porch. Mrs. Whipple answered the door. She was a stout woman with plump red cheeks and black hair woven in braids atop her head. Her apron was dusted with flour and spots of chocolate.

"Do come in," she said. "The Reverend will be delighted you're here, Nessa. We were just discussing your nuptials."

Nessa swallowed an angry reply. It upset her that he continued to talk as if they were getting married. "Mrs. Whipple," she said, keeping her voice calm, "I'm here for Mary Ellen. Is she well?"

The woman's smile faded. She disappeared into another room. "Pastor," she said, "the young lady is here to see you."

Nessa felt her temper rise. She looked at Rolly for help.

"Don't worry," he whispered, giving her hand a quick squeeze.

The minister came into the entryway. His shirt fit snugger around his middle and his chin seemed to have doubled since his arrival in Prairie River some weeks ago. "I'm happy to see you, dear," he said, reaching for her.

Nessa put her hands behind her back and turned toward the parlor. "It's Mary Ellen I came to see. Oh, there she is."

The girl was knitting by the fire.

"I've been sick," she said, without looking at her visitors. She kept her eyes on her yarn. Nessa could see she was making a pair of mittens, red and blue stripes, but noticed the pattern did not line up evenly. The stripes were crooked. For an instant she enjoyed a small satisfaction at the girl's mistake, but then felt ashamed. After all, she — Nessa — didn't know the first thing about knitting and probably wouldn't do much better herself.

The room was quiet. After a long silence Nessa said, "Well, then, guess we should go now. We just came by to say hello and bring the spelling words." Nessa unfolded a piece of paper from her sleeve.

Just then, Mrs. Whipple came in and snatched the paper from her hand. "I'll take care of this. If there's nothing else, I'll see you children to the door."

Nessa ignored the insult of being called a child. "I hope you feel better, Mary Ellen."

As they left the room, Nessa glanced back at the hearth. Mary Ellen had brought her knitting to within inches of her face and was squinting. It occurred to her that perhaps the girl hadn't been ill after all. Perhaps it was her vision that ailed her. Was that why she didn't want to read in front of others? And why she hadn't been able to see storm clouds when she came to the Locketts' that afternoon?

Reverend McDuff walked Nessa and Rolly to the door. "It was so nice to see both of you. May I count on our visiting together in church on Sunday, during the fellowship time? Mrs. Whipple has promised to bring some of her berry pies, and I'm telling you they are scrumptious."

"Oh, yes, sir," said Rolly. "I'll be there early to help set up the benches and will stay after, too. I love berry pie."

"Good. Then I'll look forward to it, son." The minister extended his hand to shake with Rolly, but Nessa turned away. She stepped outside without a word.

As she rode home in the saddle behind Rolly, she put her arms around his waist and laid her head against his back where her face was out of the wind. She closed her eyes. *Dear Jesus,* she prayed, *I'm sorry for not being nice to Reverend McDuff and for being frustrated with Mary Ellen. If You want to use me in their lives, please show me how, because I'm out of ideas and just plain tired.*

CHAPTER TWENTY-EIGHT

>>—♦—<<

An Odd Request

The following week, an idea came to Nessa. She walked to town after breakfast. The Applewoods' store was similar to Mr. Filmore's, down to the tiny bell attached to the door. It rang when Nessa stepped inside.

"Hello, Mrs. Applewood," she said to the woman behind the counter. Nessa had left Green at home because of the dog's bad habit of stealing things. Once it had been a deck of cards from a low shelf, another time a pair of soft leather gloves. Nessa didn't have enough money to keep paying for these sorts of things and did not want to risk being scolded. Without her dog, however, Nessa felt somewhat vulnerable and alone.

"You must be here for your trousseau," said Mrs. Applewood. Her mouth moved upward in an attempt to smile. It was the first outwardly friendly gesture the woman had offered Nessa since she'd arrived in Prairie River ten months earlier.

"Trousseau?" asked Nessa. The word was familiar, but she couldn't recall its meaning.

Mrs. Applewood leaned over the counter to speak to

Nessa in a low voice. "New undergarments," she said, "and other pretty things a bride should take into her marriage. The reverend will make you a fine husband."

Nessa was embarrassed by the mention of something so private. It seemed the whole town was looking forward to a wedding that only she — Nessa — was determined would not take place. She realized the reason Mrs. Applewood was being pleasant was because of the betrothal. But not wanting to argue her side of the story, Nessa changed the subject.

"Actually," she said, "I'm here about another matter, something quite important. I could really use your help."

"*Our* help?" The woman's cheeks showed a hint of color as she responded with a true smile.

At the sound of his name, Mr. Applewood had come from the back room where their rolltop desk and account books were. His spectacles were on the end of his nose and he held a pencil.

"What is it now?" he said, impatient to have been interrupted.

The usual nervousness Nessa felt when facing this couple made her throat feel dry. Her hands were at her side, hidden in the folds of her skirt.

"Sir," she began, "since you're head of the school committee, I need your advice."

He straightened his shoulders. "It's about time."

"I'm worried about one of my students." Nessa spoke rapidly to avoid being interrupted. "It's possible this girl has poor eyesight, which will hinder her education. She's smart, but she refuses to read in class. I think it's because she's embarrassed."

Nessa drew in a breath, then continued. "This is an odd request, Mr. Applewood, but may I please borrow your spectacles, to show my student? If they help her see better, maybe we could order her a pair from back East."

The man crossed his arms and regarded Nessa over the top of his eyeglasses. "What's so blame important about a girl being able to read?"

"Well, sir . . ." Nessa's mind raced with ideas, but only one seemed crucial right now. "You hired me to be the schoolteacher for Prairie River's children. I remember you saying that it's my job to make sure they can read. Boys *and* girls. Those were your words, sir."

Mr. Applewood sighed long and loud. After a moment he unhooked the wire rim of his spectacles from one ear, then another. Folding them, he set them on the counter.

"I'll need them back tomorrow," he said, "before supper. That's when I read my newspaper. Also, I have accounts to tally, you realize."

"Yes, sir . . . thank you, sir!" Nessa patted his burly hand before he had a chance to pull away, then she rushed outside. She was excited about tomorrow. And if Mary Ellen didn't show up for class, she would walk to her house after school.

Even if it did mean facing Reverend McDuff again.

CHAPTER TWENTY-NINE

The Difficult Student

That night Nessa had trouble sleeping, despite the warm comfort offered by her buffalo robe. The idea of again visiting Mrs. Whipple *and* the minister kept her awake for hours. *Why did I think I was brave enough to return to that house?*

But next morning, Nessa forgot those worries when she saw Mary Ellen in her red cloak and red hood coming across the school yard. Not until this moment had she been so glad to see the girl. Now all Nessa needed to do was find a graceful way to mention the spectacles. She rehearsed in her mind what to say, but nothing sounded right.

Good morning Mary Ellen, I notice you squint when . . .
Hello, Mary Ellen, would you like to try something new?
Mary Ellen, I thought maybe these eyeglasses could . . .

Whichever way Nessa worded her thoughts, she felt awkward, and she worried Mary Ellen would take offense, no matter what was said.

So for now, she decided to say nothing.

The wind was colder than usual so Nessa kept everyone inside for recess. From her basket she pulled out a new jump rope that she and Rolly had made, using empty spindles of thread for the handles. Her biggest student, Howard, and Rolly pushed the desks to the sides of the room so there would be open space for jumping. Then, in the corner, they started a game of marbles with Sven.

Thankful for the stove's heat, Nessa pulled up a small bench to sit as close as she could. While the younger girls skipped rope, she brought out a scrap of paper onto which she had copied down a verse last night from her father's Bible. She had read it to her students earlier, but wanted to read it again. It was from the Epistle of James.

. . . let every man be swift to hear, slow to speak, slow to wrath . . .

As Nessa reflected on its meaning, she decided she would try to listen more carefully to people and not get riled up so fast when they said things that upset her. She was relieved Ivy was helping the younger girls because she still felt awkward about bringing up the subject of the soldier. Nessa just did not know how to talk to her friend about that matter.

Now for curiosity's sake, Nessa unfolded Mr. Applewood's glasses and tried them on. The words leaped at her, as large as a headline. When she surveyed the room, the jumping girls were a blur, but when she looked back at the page, she could see clearly.

Mary Ellen sat beside her.

"Hello there," said Nessa. She removed the eyeglasses. "Want to try these? They're Mr. Applewood's, but he loaned them to me for today."

Mary Ellen was a head taller than Nessa, even sitting side by side. "Why should I want to look through the spectacles of an old man, anyway?"

"You don't have to," said Nessa. "It's just that they make reading easier."

"My mother taught me just fine, and we read together every evening, not that it's any of your business."

Nessa clenched her jaw. The Bible verse about being slow to anger flitted from her memory. Mary Ellen Whipple was impossible. Nessa stood up, wanting to distance herself from this unpleasant girl. But when she did, there was an unfortunate result.

The weight of Nessa leaving her end of the bench thrust it into the air and — like a seesaw — the other end slammed down, spilling Mary Ellen onto the floor.

A burst of giggles came from the girls, the boys smiled in silence.

"Oh, no," cried Nessa, reaching to pull the girl up. "I'm so sorry. . . . It was an accident."

"Sure it was." Mary Ellen slapped away Nessa's hand, then brushed off her dress. "You think you're so smart, but you're just an orphan with no place to belong. I'm telling Reverend McDuff about your tricks. I can't imagine why he'd be interested in a child like you."

After Nessa dismissed school for the day, there were two men she wanted to visit. Rolly agreed to escort her. Riding Buttercup together under the late afternoon sun, they first stopped at Mr. Applewood's. The wind pushed at the door as they closed it behind them, filling the store with cold air.

"Things didn't go as well as I thought they would," Nessa told the man. "I know you need your spectacles, but may I please keep them for a little while longer? Or maybe I could borrow them again later this week?"

Mr. Applewood thought a moment and then, to Nessa's surprise, said, "Guess there's no harm in your keeping them. Mr. Button's newspaper is running late anyhow, and my bookkeeping can wait a bit, I suppose."

Nessa was so delighted not to be scolded, she felt like hugging the shopkeeper, but instead called, "Thank you!" over her shoulder and ran out of the store like a schoolgirl herself.

CHAPTER THIRTY

———⟫•◊•⟪———

Another Try

Rolly and Nessa stood in the Whipples' entryway.

"Mary Ellen does not wish to see you," said the woman.

"I don't blame her for being upset," said Nessa, "but this time we came to see Reverend McDuff."

Mrs. Whipple raised an eyebrow. "Make up your mind, child. You're like the wind, changin' this way, then that. No wonder folks whisper about your state of mind and feel sorry for our pastor, poor man." She led them into the kitchen but did not invite them to sit or to warm themselves. The minister was at the table with a cup of coffee. Soup was simmering on the stove.

Nessa noticed the floor was strewn with crumbs and clods of dirt as if it hadn't been swept in a while. Unlike Mrs. Lockett's kitchen, the windows here were covered with curtains so that you couldn't see outside. The pantry shelves were nearly bare.

"We can stay only a moment," Nessa said, "but I have a kindness to ask of you, Reverend McDuff."

"Oh?" He set his cup down and sat up straight. "What might that be, dear?"

Nessa explained the day's events, then handed him the spectacles with an envelope addressed to Mary Ellen. Sealed inside was a letter she had written after school:

Dear Mary Ellen,
 I am truly sorry for embarrassing you in class today. It was an accident, honest it was. If Mr. Applewood's eyeglasses help you read this letter, he can get a pair for your very own. School will be more fun for you, and you could even help me teach the younger children to read.
Sincerely,
Nessa

As Nessa turned to leave, Reverend McDuff stood up and walked with her to the porch. "I'll talk to Mary Ellen, dear. Then on another matter entirely, may I have a word with you after church on Sunday?"

Nessa hesitated. In her head she cried, "No!" but then felt selfish. After all, he had just agreed to do something she'd asked of him. Things couldn't be her way all the time.

"Yes," she said, "of course. I'll see you in a few days."

Mrs. Lockett's barn was L-shaped. Its walls were made from layers of sod carved from the earth. A window allowed in sunlight and a view of the prairie. As Nessa brushed Wildwing's gray flanks, she listened to the wind howling outside. Though the low ceiling made the barn feel snug, there was enough room for all the animals:

Buttercup, the cow and pig, a donkey, and a cat that patrolled for mice. Green was curled up in a bed of hay.

"You're my best friends," she told her dog and colt. "I don't know what I'd do without you." Then Nessa poured out her heart. She told them about her aunt Britta and the twins, wondering aloud if she should leave Prairie River.

"My life sure would be easier," she said. "No more Reverend McDuff, or Applewoods, or Mary Ellen Whipple." Nessa hugged Wildwing's neck and began crying. At the sound of her tears, Green came over and sat on her mistress's foot, leaning into her skirt. The dog lifted a paw to shake.

"Oh, you're such a good girl," she said, taking the paw, then kneeling in the hay. Nessa buried her face in the soft yellow fur. "Don't worry, Green, I would bring you with me."

While she was kneeling, Nessa felt her colt's front leg. His overgrown hoof looked healthier since she and Rolly had been filing it. His improvement had been steady since they had rescued him from being put down by an army officer. Soon, they hoped, Wildwing would no longer limp. She patted his flank, then walked to the window to look out.

The cavalry was riding in formation toward the fort, the soldier in front carrying the Stars and Stripes. The sight of them reminded her that Fanny Jo's husband had sent word from Fort Dodge that he would be able to visit before spring.

Also, she remembered the invitation to Captain Webster's quarters for tea tomorrow afternoon. She and Ivy were finally going to meet the girl who had been rescued from Indians. Nessa looked forward to making a new friend and possibly bringing her some comfort.

But as much as she tried to think of pleasant things, Nessa's mind kept drifting ahead to Sunday.

CHAPTER THIRTY-ONE

⟨⟩

A New Friend

The next day was Saturday. Ivy and Nessa sat in Mrs. Webster's front room. It had furnishings similar to Poppy's house, but here the prickly furniture was red instead of green. This room, too, had a piano in the corner and a dirt floor with no rug.

There were so many questions Nessa wanted to ask the girl sitting opposite them. Julia Montgomery was fourteen years old, but somehow looked older. The backs of her hands and her face were tanned despite it being the middle of winter. Her brown hair, which was neatly combed atop her head, had streaks of blond in the scalp, as if she'd spent hours outside without a bonnet.

Julia's dress was blue satin with puffed sleeves that fastened at the wrists with ivory buttons. A corset shaped her waist into a tiny hourglass. She looked pinched for breath. Every time she crossed her ankles, her high-buttoned shoes showed beneath her hem.

"Excuse me," she said in a soft voice, "it's been so long since I've sat in a chair. I'm a bit restless."

The girls leaned forward, interested to hear more,

then Nessa's questions began tumbling out. "What is it like to live in a tepee? Were the Indians nice to you? What kind of food do they eat?"

Julia looked at the floor, her eyes filling with tears. Suddenly, Nessa felt foolish and ashamed of herself. How could she have forgotten that warriors had killed this girl's family?

"Oh, dear," said Nessa. "I'm sorry to upset you."

Ivy looked down at her lap. In a voice barely above a whisper she said, "This probably won't make you feel better, Julia, but we've lost our mothers, too. It's not the same as what you've been through, not at all. But we're also far from home. Like you are."

The girl blinked back her tears, her chin quivered. In a measured voice she said, "I'm so sorry to hear about your mothers. You must miss them terribly. Mama . . . I think about her every day. My sister, too, and Papa."

Nessa felt her throat tighten with thoughts of her aunt and brothers so far away. Suddenly, she burst into tears. Embarrassed by her emotions, she covered her face with her hands. After a moment she lifted her hem to wipe her cheeks, then gave a small laugh. "And here I thought I could encourage *you*, Julia."

The room was quiet except for the crackle of flames in the stove. After a moment, Julia said, "Nessa, this is a happy day for me. It's been a long time since I've been with two girls my own age, speaking English. At least a year, I reckon." She leaned toward them to whisper, while rubbing her side. "This corset is a miserable thing, and so is this poky chair. I wish we could sit on the floor, but Mrs. Webster told me it's uncivilized. She also said if I don't relearn proper manners real quick, I'll be an embarrassment to everyone."

"Tea is served," said Mrs. Webster. The captain's wife stood nearby as a young Negro girl carried in a tray. There was a clatter of cups and saucers as she set it on a low table. "Thank you, Clementine. That will be all."

The girl was about twelve years old. Her head was covered with short pigtails tied on the ends with yellow ribbons. She gave Nessa a smile of recognition before lowering her eyes in shyness.

As Nessa watched her return to the kitchen area, she recalled her last conversation with Mrs. Webster. Nessa had come to the house to invite Clementine to school.

The captain's wife had grown angry. "I'm afraid that's not possible," she had said, "my boys sitting in the same classroom as Clementine." Then she had hurried Nessa out the door, mocking her for being an orphan.

Now Nessa had another idea, which she practiced in her head for several minutes. Mrs. Webster poured tea, then offered the girls a plate of tiny sandwiches made with cheese and sweet pickles. When she seated herself, her hoopskirt filled the chair.

"Ma'am?" asked Nessa.

"Yes?"

"Julia has agreed to come to school during her stay at Fort Larned."

"Splendid," said the woman, "as long as the behavior

of your students is appropriate. Julia's ordeal is something she does not need to explain to curiosity seekers, do you understand, Nessa?"

"Yes, ma'am."

A clock on the bookcase chimed quarter past the hour.

"Since Rolly drives his sled to town to pick up Ivy, there's plenty of room for Julia," said Nessa. She paused. "And room for Clementine."

Mrs. Webster's teacup stopped in midair. Her lips tightened. "Are you defying me, young lady?"

"No, ma'am. I'm the schoolteacher, is all. I love teaching. Mr. Applewood hired me to help all of the children in Prairie River. He didn't say that only some were allowed at school and others were not."

"You're a fine one to talk, Nessa Clemens, considering you and the minister —"

"Mrs. Webster?" The voice was Julia's.

The woman's face softened as she looked at the girl. "Yes, dear?"

"I would like it very much if Clementine could accompany me to school, please. She has become a great comfort. It'll feel good to be back in class and to have friends again."

Mrs. Webster's erect posture slumped as she sighed. "I don't know," she said. "I just don't know. Captain Webster will need to decide the matter." She stood and walked over to the piano, her silk dress swishing as it brushed against the furniture. She sat on the mahogany stool and spread her skirts around her like a pleated fan. Without looking at the girls, she started playing a hymn, one of Nessa's favorites.

Remembering that tomorrow was her meeting with Reverend McDuff, Nessa took the words to heart:

Love divine, all loves excelling,
Joy of heav'n, to earth come down;
Fix in us Thy humble dwelling;
All Thy faithful mercies crown.
Jesus, Thou art all compassion;
Pure, unbounded love Thou art;
Visit us with Thy salvation;
Enter ev'ry trembling heart.

CHAPTER THIRTY-TWO

Signs from the Lord

At church on Sunday, Nessa sat in the back row between Ivy and Julia. She couldn't concentrate on Reverend McDuff's sermon because she kept wondering what he would say to her afterward.

During the closing hymn while everyone stood, Ivy gave Nessa a sympathetic look. "Do you want me to stay with you?" she whispered.

Nessa shook her head. "It's about time I stop being afraid of him. Thank you, though."

The fellowship seemed to take forever. Nessa distracted herself by greeting Mrs. Bell and her husband the blacksmith. Their baby, Oliver, crawled among the benches, then when he came to Nessa, he grabbed the cloth of her skirt, pulling himself up to stand on wobbly legs. She swooped him into her arms.

"You're such a big boy, now," she said, cuddling him. "Pretty soon you and little Kit Carson will be riding horses together." Oliver's wet diaper oozed onto Nessa's sleeves. She kissed his cheek, then handed him back to his mother.

Hoss strummed a few chords on his guitar to get everyone's attention. "Dinner's in half an hour," he said. "Me and Button are headin' home now, so see you all soon. Skies are clear."

The after-church gatherings were Nessa's favorite part of Sundays. Townsfolk took turns hosting the event and each household brought food to share. Last week had been with Lucy's family, and today's meal would be at the cousins' ranch.

Soon after Hoss's announcement, folks began gathering up picnic baskets from the back of the room and putting on their coats. Nessa found the pan of corn muffins she had baked that morning and carried them to the door, her sleeves still damp from Oliver's diaper.

Out the window she could see Rolly waiting for her by the barn, the wind blowing his hair around his face. She wanted to hurry out to him and hoped the minister had forgotten about the meeting or changed his mind. He was by the stove, talking with two of the soldiers who had attended the service.

When Mary Ellen Whipple put on her red cloak, she took the spectacles from her pocket and returned them to the storekeeper. Nessa wondered if they had helped her see better, but her thoughts were interrupted by Reverend McDuff's voice.

"Nessa, dear," he said, touching her elbow. She stepped back from the doorway to let the others leave, shivering from cold air that had invaded the room. Wind ruffled her skirt.

He waited until the door had closed behind the last person. "Well, here we are," he said.

Reverend McDuff leaned against one of the desks and crossed his arms over his stomach. "Nessa, since the day I arrived in Prairie River, I've been pleading with God for wisdom. When Mr. Carey had suggested that you and I marry, I must say I was pleased. I had been so lonely, and I had believed it was a sign from God that we should be together. That is why I followed you here. Because you're just fourteen years old, I imagined you would need me to take care of you."

Nessa studied his face for meaning. Because he rarely smiled, she couldn't tell if the lines around his eyes meant he was happy or sad. Then something occurred to her. When had his sister Lizzie died in childbirth? Was it three years ago or four? Nessa remembered the funeral, standing with Albert at the grave site, both crying. *Perhaps the minister has been melancholy since then,* she thought. He must have been lonely since losing her.

The muffins in Nessa's arms felt heavy. She held the pan close to her, to keep from dropping it. Against the tin, she could feel the beating of her heart.

"Dear girl, I've been waiting and watching for another sign from God, but when it finally came, it wasn't what I thought it would be."

Nessa had trouble finding her voice. "What do you mean?"

"Nessa, you've said *no* to me more times than I dare to count. But these past weeks, God has shown me several things quite clearly, namely that the children of Prairie River adore their schoolteacher. Your concern for Mary Ellen is exemplary, and you've earned the admiration of many folks here. That Mrs. Lockett considers you her own daughter tells me you've at last found a family. I had hoped to bring you back to Missoura with me, but I see you've made a life for yourself here, a good one."

Reverend McDuff lifted his hand as if he wanted to caress Nessa's cheek, but withdrew it. "This is hard for me to admit, but —" He took a deep breath and looked out the window. "But I think I misunderstood what God was saying. I'm so sorry, dear, for being a source of frustration to you, and I will no longer tell people we are getting married, unless you come to me and say otherwise."

All that Nessa had dreaded for so long was suddenly lifted from her shoulders. She wanted to run outside and yell for joy, but she felt light-headed and unable to speak.

"Very well then," he said, "I see Rolly is waiting for you. May I escort you to the barn? I don't want to make you late for supper." The minister took his coat from the hook and put on his mittens. They were striped red and blue. From the crooked lines, Nessa knew it was the pair knit by Mary Ellen.

"Thank you, Reverend McDuff." When he took her arm to lead her down the icy steps, she wanted to tell him how grateful and relieved she was, but no words came. She was unable to look at the man who had just touched her heart.

CHAPTER THIRTY-THREE

A Little Salt

Clouds streaked high across the sky. They were white, so Nessa wasn't concerned about a storm as she hurried along the path to town, Green trotting beside her. She had also decided not to worry about the rabid wolf. During Sunday supper, Hoss said it probably had curled up somewhere and died, on account that no one had seen it for a while.

Besides, Nessa's mind was on other things. There was so much she wanted to tell Ivy.

The sutler's cabin was warm enough for the girls to take off their shawls. Ivy had made soup from beans and sausage, which she ladled into bowls. The table was set with a blue cloth and a plate of fresh bread. An empty tin can held a bouquet of dried flowers. Nessa loved visiting her friend because she always felt so welcomed.

"Then what did you say to Reverend McDuff?" Ivy asked.

"Nothing," said Nessa. "Suddenly, I was confused, but I don't know why. When he walked me out of the schoolhouse to Rolly's sled, I felt different toward him."

Ivy sat down, folded her hands and bowed her head. *"Dear Lord, we ask You to please bless this food. Thank You, amen."* Picking up her spoon, she said, "Do you think you might want to marry him after all, when you get to know him better?"

"No!" Nessa almost shouted the word. She began buttering her bread. "I don't even want to think about marriage."

"What about Albert?"

Nessa's eyes drifted to the window. "When I think about Albert, I feel happy. I miss him because he's a good friend. But with Reverend McDuff . . . I don't know what to call it. It's just that I don't hate him anymore. And I think I might understand him better."

Ivy got up to get the saltbox sitting on a shelf. She brought it to the table and took a pinch to sprinkle in her soup. "Well, Nessa, he said some good things about you and admitted a mistake. Maybe you respect him for that. But pardon me for saying this, he could add a little spice to his sermons."

Nessa laughed. She pinched some salt and made a dramatic show of adding it to her soup. "I fall asleep."

"Me, too," said Ivy. "But I bet he'll be more interesting now that he's trying hard to listen to the Lord."

Nessa took a spoonful of soup, then another. "This is good, Ivy."

"Thank you." Ivy brought a napkin to her lips and lowered her voice. "Nessa, when you talk about Albert being your good friend, that you feel glad to see him, well, that's how I feel every time Penn comes into the store."

"That soldier . . . Pennsylvania Lee?"

Ivy nodded. "The yellow stripe on his pants means he rides with the cavalry. On Sunday he walked me home from the church supper. It was a long way, but Papa gave us permission."

"You hardly know him," said Nessa.

"But I want to. How else can you know someone if you don't spend time together?"

Nessa sighed with exasperation. "But why a soldier? He could get ambushed by some of those Indians who don't want peace. It's dangerous riding out on the prairie."

"Who else, Nessa? There're no senators out here in the middle of nowhere or college professors. I'm a sutler's daughter. Papa knows soldiers and does business with them every day. Besides, Penn is close to a promotion."

"*Promotion?* That's just another word for 'transfer.'" Nessa felt like crying. The reason Fanny Jo's husband was no longer at Fort Larned was because he had been promoted to lieutenant, then reassigned to Fort Dodge.

Nessa didn't know how to express the emotions that now flooded her. She had come to Prairie River to get away from a marriage. After a rough start, she finally had a new life and a true friend. But now this friend might be taken away from her by the very thing Nessa had been trying to avoid in the first place. Her head hurt from trying to sort through it all.

But another matter was troubling her. What if Ivy weren't the one to leave?

"Ivy, what would you think if I wrote my aunt Britta and told her I was coming to Wisconsin to live with her?"

"Are you teasing?"

"No."

"Nessa, I would cry my eyes out to think I might never see you again."

Nessa looked at her friend, swallowing hard to keep from crying. She was touched and overwhelmed by the depth of their friendship. She hoped nothing would come between them.

CHAPTER THIRTY-FOUR

The Recipe

As soon as Nessa dried the supper dishes, she lit a candle to take upstairs. Mrs. Lockett, the sisters, Minnie, and Rolly were lingering in the warm kitchen over apple cobbler and cups of cocoa. Fanny Jo was in the rocking chair, nursing baby Kit.

"Good night, everyone," Nessa said. "I'm tired and tomorrow's school."

"Sweet dreams, darlin'," said Mrs. Lockett. "Laura and I'll be gettin' breakfast in the mornin', so stay in bed as long as you like. We'll wake you when the hotcakes are comin' off the griddle."

Nessa opened her trunk. Stacked at the bottom were folders containing her mother's drawings, bundles of letters, and an assortment of books. She still hadn't examined some of the items since first discovering the trunk. This time she was curious about something covered in red cloth. To her surprise, it was a cookbook written in a foreign language. Danish, she guessed.

She wished she could understand the inscription in the front page, but did recognize her grandmother's name as the same she'd seen in the family Bible. The date was 25 December 1851. It appeared to have been a Christmas gift to Nessa's mother. At the time, Nessa would have been eight months old.

As she flipped through the recipes, she noticed several blank pages in back that had been filled with handwritten notes. On one of them was a pencil sketch of a young girl about two years old, sitting on a porch step. Her hair curled to her chin and her head was tilted slightly as if smiling into the sun. The initials, ccc, were scripted into a clump of grass that touched the child's bare foot. Immediately, Nessa knew the artist had been her mother, Claire Christine Clemens.

And at the bottom of the page, written in the same hand, was what Nessa assumed was a personal recipe. But upon reading it, Nessa realized it was actually a prayer, and the drawing was a portrait of herself at age two.

For my daughter Vanessa, a prayer, upon the occasion of her second birthday:

Whatever things are true,
Whatever things are honest,
Whatever things are just,
Whatever things are pure,
Whatever things are lovely,
Whatever things are of good report:

If there be any virtue, and
If there be any praise,
Think on these things. — Philippians 4:8

Tears welled up, but Nessa brushed them away so she could study the picture. *This is what my mother saw when she looked at me. A smiling pretty baby.* Nessa looked more closely and noticed a dimple under the left cheekbone. She jumped off her bed to look in the mirror. Staring at her reflection, she gasped with surprise. There it was, a dimple! Why hadn't she seen it before? And why hadn't anyone ever mentioned it?

Nessa brought the cookbook to her face and sniffed deeply, as if by doing so she could catch a scent of her mother's kitchen and her grandmother's cooking. Again she read the prayer.

Oh, Lord, thank You for a mother who wanted such beauty for me. Nessa's heart was so full of gratitude she knelt on the cold floor to pray. When she pulled her buffalo robe over her shoulders, Green crept underneath the fur and lay at her side.

As she began thanking God for everything she could think of, she remembered the minister and his apology.

Lord Jesus, I'm sorry for having hated Reverend McDuff, and if I've done anything wrong that I don't know about yet, I'm sorry for that, too. Please bless him with a bride who will bring him happiness. He deserves someone who will truly love him. And, Lord, please show me how to be kind without misleading him. . . .

With tender care, Nessa returned the cookbook to her trunk, closed the lid, then blew out her candle. She crawled into bed, patting the spot beside her until Green jumped up.

At long last, Nessa was looking forward to church next Sunday and being able to greet Reverend McDuff as her pastor. Hugging her dog for warmth, she soon fell asleep.

CHAPTER THIRTY-FIVE

Change of Plans

Nessa stood in front of her students, beaming with pride.

Eleven, she counted, now the second day in a row. They brushed the snow off their shoes, hung up their coats in the entryway, then stored lunch pails by their seats so the food wouldn't freeze. Earlier, the boys had helped Hoss unload the day's supply of buffalo chips and firewood brought from his ranch. It now was stacked neatly in a corner. A bucket of water was heating on the stove. Bonnie Prince Charlie and Buttercup were safe in the barn.

How happy Nessa was to see Clementine walk up the path with Julia, arm in arm. The two sat in back on the same bench with Ivy and Mary Ellen. At first, the others were reserved upon seeing the Negro girl in school, but soon warmed up as they observed Julia's and Ivy's open acceptance of her, and of course Nessa's.

Nessa greeted each student by name. The youngest — Lucy, Augusta, Poppy, and Minnie — were in the front row, whispering. In a moment, Nessa would ask them to be quiet so class could begin.

The boys filled the middle row. Big Howard, Rolly, and Sven were passing something among themselves that captivated their interest. Nessa walked to their row.

"What on earth is that?" she asked.

"Green brought it to us," said Big Howard. He jutted his chin in the direction of Green's blanket, where the dog was sleeping on her back, paws in the air.

The girls in the front row had stopped whispering and turned around to look. "Eew," they said in unison.

The object appeared to be a flat rock the size of a shoe.

"It's dead," said Rolly. "Poor ol' snapping turtle. Green dug it up from a pile of leaves by the creek when we went for water. It took forever before we could pry it out of her mouth."

Nessa examined the shell without touching, because it had a stink of dead fish. At the openings where the turtle would have pulled in its legs and head for protection, there was dried mud.

Sven took a stick from his pocket and began scraping out the interior. Nessa didn't want to discourage their curiosity, so she let the discovery continue. As dirt sprinkled onto the floor, she glanced out the window. Blue sky. But when she looked out the opposite window, she saw a black cloud on the horizon. Knowing how quickly blizzards could devour the prairie, she became concerned. There was only enough wood to last through the afternoon. She remembered the storm on Minnie's birthday, how for three days and two nights they had been snowed in.

Alarmed, but not wanting to frighten her students, she went over to the window to better see out. Streaks of gray and white were spreading over the prairie. Indeed, a storm was coming, but it seemed far enough away for them to get home in time.

Sven was holding up the empty turtle shell. "See, I told you it was dead." With a proud smile he turned around in his seat and showed it to Mary Ellen. She shook her head with disapproval.

"If *I* were schoolteacher," she said, "this sort of nonsense would not be tolerated."

Nessa felt herself bristle at the insult. Ordinarily, she would take advantage of this moment for teaching. They could have a vigorous discussion about how different animals prepare for winter. She wanted to show Mary Ellen the value of studying nature, but at the moment was too unsettled by the darkening sky. Her lessons planned for the day would have to wait. Even the Bible verse she'd copied last night would stay in her pocket for now.

Being trapped in the schoolhouse would be disastrous. Since some of the children lived on nearby ranches or in dugouts by the river, it would take too long to make sure they were all safely home. In an instant, Nessa decided they should take shelter together at the boardinghouse. They could get there faster and — should the blizzard last into the night — there would be enough firewood to keep them from freezing. And, of course, Mrs. Lockett's full pantry would keep them from hunger.

Nessa clapped her hands to get their attention. "There's a storm," she said. "It looks like it's far off, so we have time to head for town. We'll stay together and wait it out at the Locketts'. Rolly, could you and Howard please get the horses ready and the sled?"

Without answering, the two boys rushed for their coats and scarves, put on hats and mittens, then ran outside. Cold wind roared into the room before Nessa was able to push the door closed. The sudden chill in the schoolhouse frightened her. Was the blizzard moving faster than she thought?

From the window she watched the boys run for the barn, counting the seconds in her head. "... Six ... seven ... eight ... nine." They were in. When they closed the wide wooden door behind them, Nessa breathed a sigh of relief. The distance between the two buildings was no more than that between Mrs. Lockett's house and barn, but now seemed much farther.

She turned to her students. "Let's get ready. Front row first. In an orderly fashion, please, you may go get your things." As the younger girls walked to the entryway, Nessa noticed Green with her nose in the air, sniffing. The fur on her neck was standing up straight. The dog growled low in her throat.

"What is it, girl?" asked Nessa. She again looked at the barn.

But what she saw filled her with terror. She pressed her fingers to her mouth to keep from crying out.

Three wolves were pacing in front of the barn. They were gray and thin with long legs, like the one Fanny Jo had described seeing. The one with rabies.

Nessa's mouth felt too dry to speak. She stared out, trying to think of what to do. Minnie came to her side. Her gaze followed Nessa's.

"My brother's out there," she said. Her voice was trembling.

"He'll be all right," said Nessa, pretending a confidence she didn't feel. "There's a window so they can see out. I'm sure they'll stay inside until it's safe."

"But the storm —" Minnie leaned into Nessa's skirt and looked up at her with big eyes.

The storm worried Nessa, too, but the wolves upset her even more. She faced her students, her arm around Minnie. "May I have your attention, please? There's been a change of plans."

CHAPTER THIRTY-SIX

Waiting

Within minutes, the storm became a tempest, filling the sky with blowing snow. The thick sod walls of the schoolhouse held fast, but the windows rattled and leaked cold air. The sills were two feet wide, which was where Nessa leaned on her elbows to watch the barn. The wolves were still there.

Lord, please don't let the boys open that door —

A scream from one of the girls interrupted her prayer. Nessa hurried over to where Lucy was pointing outside.

A wolf was looking up at them, its head inches away from the bottom of the window. Nessa pulled the youngest children away and ushered them to the center of the room, by the stove. Green circled the group, her fur on end.

"Stay here," she said. "If the wolves can't see us, they'll go away." Nessa didn't know if this was true, but it sounded true. She didn't want her students to be as terrified as she now was. The stories she'd heard about these wild animals made her feel sick with dread. They were fast and could jump high, breaking through windows if they were starving.

Whether or not these wolves were rabid or just hungry didn't matter to Nessa. Rolly and Howard were trapped in the barn without a fire to warm themselves, and without any food. She felt desperate knowing there was nothing she could do to help.

The afternoon wore on. Green continued to whine and walk from window to window. Nessa enlisted the help of the older girls to play games with the others. She abandoned the idea of teaching when she saw how drowsy and distracted everyone was. She had lost all sense of time because of not being able to see anything out the windows except gray, white, and more gray. When a headache began nagging her, she realized she was hungry and that the children must be, too.

They gathered near the stove and opened their lunch pails. At the sight of food, Green politely lifted her paw to show her interest, but then returned to pacing the room.

Nessa saw the children looking at the boys' pails. "Don't worry," she said. "Rolly and Howard are smart and will take good care of each other, you'll see. There's a trough of water in the barn and plenty of hay for them to cover themselves."

Nessa broke off part of her sandwich and returned the rest to her pail. "We must only eat half of our meal, in case we need to make it last for supper, too." When she bowed her head and folded her hands, so did the others.

After praying, Nessa looked up. "Would anyone else like to pray?"

Poppy in her small voice said, *"Jesus, please make the wolves go back to their own dens."*

"Watch over Mama and Papa," came another prayer.

"Lord, bless Howard and Rolly," said another. *"Let the horses keep them warm."*

As her students took turns praying, Nessa felt peaceful. She was proud of their courage. When it came time to eat, not only did they save back half of their food, they each saved a bite for Green.

Nessa kept getting up to look out the windows, hoping the wolves had gone. Green followed her every step. One thought reassured her. Because of all the times Rolly had scolded her about the weather, she knew he wouldn't dare leave the barn if he couldn't see where he was going, especially if he thought the wolves might still be there. She knew Rolly would be careful.

Even so, Nessa couldn't stop thinking about the boys being alone. It was her fault. If only she had seen the wolves, she never would have let them leave the schoolhouse. If only one of them had had a gun.

Suddenly, she felt exhausted. As the wind lashed the schoolhouse, the room grew dark except for glowing embers showing through slits in the stove's iron door. The children huddled together on the floor after having arranged benches on their sides to form a low barrier between them and the drafty windows. They drank warm water from the pot. Every coat, hat, and woolen scarf was put on, including mittens. The only blanket was Green's, which Nessa used to cover the youngest girls as they nestled together like kittens.

Because it was not possible to get to the outhouse, Nessa let Sven and Ivy make a small private area from upturned desks in a corner. They pulled up a short plank of wood, exposing the frozen dirt below. It was a primitive arrangement, but at least the children could take turns relieving themselves there.

Nessa put Julia and Clementine in charge of keeping the fire going. Now she wished she had kept Reverend McDuff's watch, to know what time it was. It felt like midnight, but maybe it was only four in the afternoon. Her stomach tightened with hunger, and she felt sleepy.

Sometime later she awoke, chilled and shivering. Her arms and legs ached from being curled up tight. The wind still howled and she could hear snow swishing against the windows. It was so cold in the room she could see her breath in the dim light. With her heart in her throat she roused each student to make sure no one had frozen to death, then got up to look in the wood box. Only a few clumps of buffalo droppings and twigs remained.

Too sleepy and too cold to pray with words, her heart begged God to help them. She was thankful to see how Julia had instructed the older girls to each cuddle one of the younger girls to help keep warm. The bad weather didn't seem to bother Julia. Nessa wondered if her months with the Cheyenne had made her braver than she —

Nessa — now felt. She put the last kindling in the stove, watched until a small flame flared up, then lay back down with Green.

She stared up at the low ceiling, where the fire reflected against the wooden beams. She was relieved that Mary Ellen hadn't blamed her for their predicament, or at least was keeping her thoughts to herself.

The sounds of the children breathing while they slept was the only thing that comforted Nessa.

CHAPTER THIRTY-SEVEN

Winter Song

A softening of the wind awoke Nessa. She bolted up-right and hurried to the window. Snow was still blowing sideways, but she could see a dark blur outside. The barn!

Hopeful that the storm was ending, she strained to better see the image. Maybe she could run and get to the boys. But to her distress the barn once again disappeared behind a veil of snow. She knew if she opened the door to call them, what little heat was left in the room would be sucked outside.

In despair, she looked out the window. What hour of day it was, she couldn't tell. All she knew was that she was cold, the children were cold.

"Sven," she said, shaking the boy's shoulder to wake him up. "You have my permission to break apart the stools and chairs for the fire."

As the boy fed in the wooden legs and backs, the warmth began to spread from the stove to the circle of benches. Nessa directed everyone to sit closely together and open their lunch pails.

"This time," she said, "we must eat just a few bites.

Chew ever so slowly. I'm sorry, everyone. I know you're hungry. So am I." The sight of Rolly and Howard's untouched food made her throat tighten. *They've had nothing to eat for . . . how long has it been?* She would save their portions in case the weather cleared and they would be able to dash back to the schoolhouse.

She felt a rising panic, but knew she must stay calm for the children. She was their teacher.

Then she remembered the verse in her pocket. It was one she read often, from Psalm 18. Because Nessa had made it a song in her head, she had quickly memorized the words.

When she started humming the tune, Minnie sat up straight. "You sing that in your room, Nessa. I've heard you."

"That's right. It cheers me up." Nessa wrapped her scarf high around her neck to keep warm. "If we think about how much God cares for us, we'll feel better. Even if we're cold and hungry." Then she sang:

> *I will love thee, O Lord, my strength.*
> *The Lord is my rock, and my fortress, and my deliverer;*
> *my God my strength, in whom I will trust . . .*
> *I will call upon the Lord, who is worthy to be praised . . .*
> *The Lord liveth; and blessed be my rock; and let the God of*
> *my salvation be exalted.*

Soon the children joined in, their voices soft, as if they were about to fall asleep.

After they had sung it twice, Nessa asked, "What do these words mean to you?"

A moment passed.

Poppy raised her hand.

"Yes, Poppy? You can keep your hand inside your coat."

"God is here with us right now."

"Yes, He is."

Lucy said, "When we're afraid, we can call on Him."

"And our souls are safe with Him," said Augusta, "no matter what kind of danger we're in."

The low flames crackled inside the stove. A gust of wind seized the schoolhouse with a tremor. Nessa looked at her students sitting in the cold shadows of their circle. She wondered if Mary Ellen was going to say anything, but no comment came.

"Well done," said Nessa. "We've called on Him and now we wait." Grateful for the darkness, she didn't want them to see how their faith had moved her to tears.

Nessa still didn't know what time of day or night it was. Her back hurt from sitting on the floor, for now only one bench remained and the desks. Without a saw, she didn't know how they would be able to feed the larger furniture into the stove's opening.

She closed her eyes and lay down. The song from earlier was still in her head, the words comforting her. *The Lord liveth; and blessed be my rock* ... A moment passed — or had it been hours? — when she awoke to a new sound. A swishing. But it wasn't from the storm, it was in the room. She leaned on her elbow and squinted in the pale firelight to see what it was.

Green was sitting at attention, staring at the door. Her tail was wagging so hard, it brushed across the floor like a broom. Then came voices, shouts from outside, and a pounding. Nessa stood up and walked as if in a dream to the entryway.

"Hello?" she called. Her breath formed a white cloud in front of her face.

"Nessa!" It was Mr. Button. "Are the children all right?"

She threw herself at the door, trying to pull it open. "Yes, yes," she cried, "but Howard and Rolly are in the barn. Please go there first."

The sound of thumping told her that someone outside was digging through snow to get the door open. She ran to a window, but it was coated inside with ice, and when she scratched at the glass, she realized that the outer pane was also glazed over.

Ivy scraped at a window that faced town. "Look. Nessa, come here."

Nessa leaned into the deep sill and peered through the small clearing that Ivy had made. She could see outside. The sky was black but lit with stars, brilliant twinkling stars that reflected onto the snowy landscape. But most beautiful was the trail of lantern light coming toward the schoolhouse. She could make out the shapes of wagons and men on horseback.

"Thank You, dear Lord," she whispered.

CHAPTER THIRTY-EIGHT

The Stage out of Town

"What about the boys?" Nessa asked Mr. Button when he finally came in the entryway.

"Soldiers are digging out the barn right now," he answered. "Come on, let's get these little ones into Hoss's wagon. He's got hot stones with furs to cover them up. And your Mrs. Lockett is waiting with hot soup. She's been beside herself, wouldn't you know it? We all have been."

Nessa stood outside on the step while her students were helped into sleds. The wind had dropped to a breeze, but the air was so icy it stung her cheeks. High drifts of snow shrouded the barn and walls of the schoolhouse. She watched as Howard's father and his uncle, Mr. Applewood, struggled to drag open the barn door wide enough to squeeze inside. As they did, Nessa held her breath. Her chest hurt with anxiety. *Lord, please let Rolly and Howard be all right.*

But soon there came an excited shout. The boys were on their feet, the horses, too.

When Rolly walked out with a fur robe around his

shoulders, then Big Howard, Nessa burst into tears of relief. She no longer cared if anyone saw her cry.

Mrs. Lockett's kitchen was crowded with friends and
concerned townsfolk. Nessa, Ivy, Minnie, and Rolly sat
together in front of the blazing stove. Their feet were in
the bathtub, which was filled with hot water up to their
shins. As the water cooled, Laura and Fanny Jo ladled it
out, then added more from the steaming kettle. This was
the quickest way for the four of them to warm up.

Nessa was so sleepy, she could hardly keep her eyes
open. She overheard Mr. Applewood say it was five
o'clock in the morning and that he had just come from
milking the cow in Mrs. Lockett's barn. He was helping
with chores and wanted to make sure the children would
have fresh milk for breakfast.

The blizzard had trapped them in the schoolhouse for
just one day and one night, but to Nessa it had seemed
forever. She wanted to crawl under her buffalo robe to
sleep, but she didn't want to go upstairs. The warm kitchen
and the friends who were caring for her filled her with
deep contentment. The storm was over, her students
were safe.

Rolly was more awake than ever. He repeated his story
of survival to each newcomer who sat down at the table
for cinnamon rolls and coffee.

". . . Then we could hear the wolves pawing at the
door," he said. "The water trough had dirt frozen on top,
but we broke the ice and drank some, anyway." Nessa listened to him describe how they burrowed into the hay to

keep warm, how the horses lay next to them. The boys ate some of the oats and carrot stubs that had been stored in burlap sacks.

"I'm starved, sure enough," Rolly said. "I still can't believe Nessa saved our dinner pails for us."

Just then, Hoss came in the back door, his hair stiff as a hairbrush, his cheeks red. Snow was on his pant legs. "I just come from the Whipples'," he said. "Mary Ellen is doin' fine. Her folks sent regards and farewell on behalf of the preacher."

The room fell silent.

"Where's he going?" asked Ivy's father.

Hoss searched the faces of everyone at the table and those standing. "You mean, you haven't heard?"

Mrs. Lockett handed him a cup of hot coffee. "Better have a seat, Hoss. What're you tryin' to tell us?"

The big cousin lowered his head. A puddle was forming on the floor as the snow melted from his boots. "Here's what," he said. "Remember that lull in the storm after supper? Well, Mrs. Whipple said that's when the minister set out for town to catch the stage. The next one wouldn't be leaving for another week or so, depending on weather."

Hoss looked at Nessa. Her feet were still in hot water, a blanket over her shoulders. He gave her a nod of respect as if to say he understood there would be no wedding. "The reverend had his return ticket," Hoss continued, "for going home to Missoura. Evidently, he wanted to start his journey before winter set in too deep."

Fanny Jo laid her baby in the cradle. "Laura, didn't he

say something to you about getting back to his congregation? His three-month rotation was up?"

"Why, yes," said her sister. "That's what he told Mrs. Bell and me last Sunday at dinner. But we didn't think he meant right away, we assumed there'd be plenty of time to plan a party, you know, send him off with all our good wishes. He had arrived only before Christmas."

A shuffling of feet came from the parlor. Mr. Applewood and Ivy's father were putting on their coats and heading for the door. The other men did the same. Hoss used one of Mrs. Lockett's clean dish towels to wipe up the puddle at his feet, then set his empty cup on the table. He adjusted his suspenders as he and his cousin stood.

"Well," said Mr. Button, "time to get back to work. Thanks for the coffee, Vivian. Good and hot as usual. I just thank the Lord all the kids are safe. We're proud of you, Nessa, honey."

"Yes, indeed," said Mrs. Lockett. She put her hand on Nessa's shoulder.

Cold air rushed into the kitchen as the men filed out onto the porch. Wind slammed the door, muffling their retreating steps. The silence hurt Nessa's ears. She felt sick to her stomach.

Reverend McDuff had left town! He hadn't said good-bye, and it was her fault. Last Sunday while helping wash dishes in Mr. Button's kitchen, no one mentioned he was leaving. But then maybe Nessa hadn't been listening. Her thoughts had been far away. She hadn't been able to stop puzzling over the good news he had told her earlier.

Was that why Mrs. Applewood had been harsh with Nessa, grabbing a plate from her hands while she was drying it? What was it some of the ladies had been whispering?

Nessa was too weary to consider how the townsfolk might now accuse her. She watched Mrs. Lockett go into the pantry for a basket of eggs, then begin cracking them one by one into a bowl. While she beat them into a froth, Laura filled the large skillet with sausage patties. Fanny Jo took another pan of cinnamon rolls from the oven. Their voices were soft as they talked among themselves.

For once, Nessa didn't jump up to help in this ritual of cooking. Exhaustion settled over her as she pulled the blanket tight around her. Her neck ached and she felt chilled.

For so many months she had hoped the minister would disappear from her life, but because of his humble apology, she no longer felt that way. The idea of Reverend McDuff traveling across the prairie without Nessa having said a kind word to him now tormented her.

And now the only person in Prairie River who had known her from childhood was gone.

CHAPTER THIRTY-NINE

—◆◆◆—

"Worth More than Many Sparrows"

For now, school was held at the fort's library. Though the room was small for twelve students, it was warm and Nessa felt safe. Should another blizzard come while they were in class, help would be there right away.

On Sunday, church was held in Mr. Filmore's store with folks sitting on benches around the stove. Hoss played an opening hymn on his guitar, then Mr. Button stood up in front by the counter to give the devotional. His bushy mustache was combed over his cheeks. He looked dignified in his blue shirt even though there were gaps in his vest where it fastened over his large stomach.

"'Mornin', folks," began Mr. Button. "We're amiss our preacher now that he's on his journey back to Missoura. Meantime, we'll just keep gathering together like always.

"Anyhow, last night when I was praying, this scripture from Matthew came to mind, so here it is: Jesus said that even though two sparrows are sold for just one penny, our Father in Heaven cares so much about these tiny birds that He knows when each one will fall to the ground. Another thing Jesus said in this same passage is that the very hairs on our head are numbered, but we don't need to fear death because we are worth more than many sparrows. For those of us who have given our hearts to Him, He has prepared a place in Heaven for us."

Mr. Button looked up at the ceiling for a moment. "What I'm trying to say here, folks, is that God loves us, and He will not forget us. Let's praise the Lord."

Hoss came to the front and began strumming chords to the familiar hymn.

How sweet the name of Jesus sounds in a believer's ear!
It soothes his sorrows, heals his wounds,
And drives away his fear.
It makes the wounded spirit whole,
And calms the troubled breast;
'Tis manna to the hungry soul,
And to the weary, rest. . . .
Jesus! My Savior, Shepherd, Friend,
My Prophet, Priest, and King,
My Lord, My Life, My Way, My End,
Accept the praise I bring. . . .

Snowdrifts still banked the schoolhouse the following week when Nessa and Rolly rode Buttercup out to have a look. Townsfolk had repaired the broken floorboard and cleaned out the dirt below. The fort's carpenter was building new stools and benches. Even though Nessa's classroom would soon be back to normal, she couldn't shake a feeling of winter blues.

She watched as the harsh winds kept changing the

shapes of the drifts. How she longed for spring and to see wildflowers in bloom. She couldn't wait until once again she and her students would sit by the creek and watch birds building their nests.

I know, she thought, *what we all need is a picnic!*

One Saturday at the beginning of March, sleigh bells rang across the frozen prairie as Rolly drove the older girls to the schoolhouse. Green rode on the seat next to him. The occasion was a get-together Nessa had planned, just for fun and for the girls to become better acquainted.

She was thrilled that Mrs. Webster let Clementine accompany Julia. The captain's wife had said yes only after realizing the outing would bring happiness to the orphaned girl. Also in the sled was Ivy in a fur bonnet and Mary Ellen, wearing her red cloak.

Wind had worn down the taller drifts by the barn and exposed dirt on the sunny side of the schoolhouse. Tracks from rabbits and deer marked the mottled ground.

"I'll be back in two hours," Rolly called as he drove away. He had stayed long enough to build a fire in the stove and study the horizon. No clouds, no wolves.

The girls spread a blanket on the floor, then unloaded their baskets. While a pot of water heated for tea, they filled their plates with fried chicken and salted potato slices that had been fried in butter. Mary Ellen passed around a jar of crunchy sweet pickles, then Clementine opened a wooden box and pulled out a small chocolate cake. It was square with dribbles of white icing, just enough for the five of them.

"Baked it this mornin'," she said. "Miz Webster let me bring it to share."

It made Nessa happy to see Julia more relaxed than during their formal visit in the Websters' parlor. She wasn't wearing a corset, and she sat with her legs crossed under her dress, not to the side as did the other girls. Her hair had been brushed into two braids, tied on the ends with string, not twirled up in combs. Nessa wondered if Mrs. Webster had allowed the changes, or if Julia had insisted on dressing as she pleased. She also wondered if Julia had yet received mail from family members, but did not want to embarrass her by asking.

After they had eaten, Nessa let Green outside while they gathered up the dishes. She would wait until Rolly arrived with the sled before putting out the fire.

As she shook out the blanket and began folding it, Ivy came over to whisper in her ear. "Come see what your dog's got this time."

Nessa remembered the dead turtle, playing cards, and other items Green had retrieved. She hoped it wasn't anything harmful. She peered out from the wide windowsill and could see her dog loping toward the door with something colorful dangling from her mouth.

Nessa's heart began to race. It was a red-and-blue mitten.

CHAPTER FORTY

Too Late

$\mathcal{N}$essa and the girls followed Green's tracks to the shady side of the barn. There they found a tall drift that had begun to melt. Nessa stared in horror.

Reverend McDuff was sitting inches away from the sod wall, his arms around his knees. His eyes were closed. Snow covered his head and back like a thick white cape. A valise was at his side.

Mary Ellen began weeping. She held the soggy mitten that she had knit for the preacher, the one Green had retrieved. Turning to Nessa she cried, "This is all your fault, you stupid girl. He was probably coming here to say good-bye. If only you weren't so selfish, this poor man would not have died with a broken heart."

Nessa felt as if the breath had been knocked from her. She didn't know how to respond to Mary Ellen's fury, nor what to do about their grisly discovery. Stunned, she clung to Ivy's arm and said a silent prayer.

The ringing of Rolly's sleigh bells came while the girls

were still huddled in their shawls, the wind blowing their skirts behind them. He ran to the scene.

"Oh, no," he said, removing his cap to show respect.

Rolly returned to town for help while the girls waited in the warmth of the schoolhouse. The wind had picked up and the air was growing colder as the sun sunk lower in the sky.

Nessa tried to imagine the minister trudging through the storm. How terrifying it must have been to lose sight of the schoolhouse, then try to find it with outstretched hands. In that blizzard, even if the wall were just inches away, he wouldn't have been able to see it.

The thought of him suffering filled her with anguish. If only he had stayed beside Mrs. Whipple's warm hearth.

Mr. Button and several men arrived from town. They dug Reverend McDuff from the snow, covered his frozen form with a blanket, then carried him to a sleigh. Nessa and Ivy watched out the window, crying silent tears.

Later that night, Nessa put a shawl over her nightgown and went to the doorway of Mrs. Lockett's room. The woman was sitting by her window knitting, a quilt around her shoulders. An oil lamp on the bureau cast golden light up the walls, which flickered from a draft. Wind outside groaned through the eaves.

"Come in, dear." Mrs. Lockett patted the end of her bed, inviting her to sit.

Nessa's sigh was full of tears. She put her hand over

her eyes, rubbing them. After a moment, she began de-
scribing Reverend McDuff's last words to her. In the
weeks since the blizzard she hadn't spoken of the encounter, except for the few details she had confided to
Ivy.

"I feel so guilty," she said. "If only I hadn't avoided him
at the church supper, maybe he would have changed his
mind about leaving Prairie River. But I was selfish, all I
could think of was my relief that he wasn't going to
bother me anymore about marriage. Mrs. Lockett, he
was a decent man, it turns out. Lonely, is all. After time
we even could have become friends. If only I —"

"Honey, listen to me." Mrs. Lockett put her knitting
in its basket and came to sit on the bed beside Nessa. She
brushed aside a lock of Nessa's hair, touching her cheek
with tenderness. "It ain't your fault he set out in a blizzard or that he came all the way to Prairie River in the
first place."

"But why did he have to die? And why didn't I get a
chance to tell him that I was grateful we'd worked out
our misunderstandings?"

Mrs. Lockett put her arm around Nessa. "I don't
know, my dear. Some things we'll have to wait till we get
to heaven to find out."

CHAPTER FORTY-ONE

The Gift

On the morning of the funeral, the skies were clear and blue. The wind had a scent of moist earth, and a chittering of birds came from the creek. Spring was beginning to awaken the prairie.

At the cemetery, soldiers had dynamited a hole in the ground, large enough to fit the minister's shrouded body. Because wood was scarce, there was no coffin.

Mr. Applewood approached Nessa after the service and handed her a small leather pouch. He cleared his throat. "This was found in the minister's vest pocket," he said. "There's a note inside. It's for you. Despite all the pain you caused this good man, he still was able to turn the other cheek, like all good Christians should."

Nessa closed her fingers around the pouch and drew in a deep breath. *Like all good Christians . . .* The words stung.

As she fought feelings of guilt, she looked out over the prairie. She was standing on the knoll by Peter's grave, where the tree planted in his memory had taken root. It had withstood winter's harsh winds, and its bare branches showed promise of coming buds. For miles around, as far as she could see, the ground held patches of melting snow. The Santa Fe Trail was dotted with puddles of mud reflecting sunlight like tiny mirrors. From a bend in the river, sandhill cranes took flight with noisy squawks. High overhead a line of geese flew in formation.

Finally, thought Nessa, *winter's almost over.* As the townsfolk wandered back to their homes, she opened the pouch. The watch with its elegant silver chain spilled into her palm, followed by a piece of folded stationery.

She held the paper tight against the wind so it wouldn't blow away.

Nessa dear,

Since we are friends and not betrothed, I trust you'll believe me when I say — once again — I truly want you to have this. As you know, my sister, Lizzie, adored you and would have heartily approved of it becoming yours. Maybe you remember she was a schoolteacher, too? One of Missouri's finest.

Nessa, I'm returning to Independence with the hope that the Lord will allow me to lead my congregation as before, despite my folly of having misunderstood Him and having embarrassed you and myself. I just wanted to stop by your classroom this afternoon and say good-bye in person. By the time you read this I'll be on the stage heading east, with a prayer in my heart for your continued well-being. May we meet again soon.

Yours faithfully,

Reverend Michael James McDuff

Nessa tried to picture the minister writing this letter at Mrs. Whipple's kitchen table, then tucking it into his pocket. Apparently, he had planned to ask Nessa to wait until school was out before reading it and finding his gift. How she wished he were here right now so she could thank him. It touched her deeply that he had wanted to share with her the memory of his sister, someone he had held so dear.

She slipped the chain over her neck. The watch hung beside her heart like a pendulum. *It's beautiful,* she thought. With her thumb, she clicked open the silver lid and held it to her ear. Someone must have wound it because the second hand was ticking and it read half past ten. She snapped the lid shut and headed for home.

As she came to the far end of the cemetery, she noticed Mr. and Mrs. Applewood near a cluster of graves. The storekeeper had removed his hat and bowed his head. Mrs. Applewood was kneeling, brushing the snow from two small headstones. After a moment he helped his wife up and took her hand, holding her close.

Nessa hurried down the path to the creek before the couple might see her. Their intimate moment had brought fresh tears to her eyes.

Whose graves? she wondered. *Had they buried a child? Or two?* Nessa was overcome with emotion, grieving anew for Reverend McDuff and now for the Applewoods' apparent loss. Nothing seemed simple anymore.

CHAPTER FORTY-TWO

———◆———

Faith Looks Up

As the snow continued to melt, Nessa looked forward to spring. The wind was still too cold to be outside for long, and the old-timers warned that in years before, blizzards had struck as late as May.

Even so, Nessa felt she had passed through a long season of uncertainty. It surprised her that her grief for Reverend McDuff wouldn't go away. Since he was the only one in Prairie River who had known her at the orphanage, she wished more than ever that he was still here. She was thankful that the last time they spoke, no harsh words had passed between them. She confided these things to Mrs. Lockett one afternoon as the woman was teaching her to knit. They were upstairs, sitting by a window to catch the remaining sunlight.

"It's time to go forward with your life, my dear," she said. Mrs. Lockett's needles clicked and paused, clicked and paused, as she looped the yarn in place.

Nessa watched the woman's strong hands as she pulled on the ball of yarn to loosen it. "Here, honey, you try." She transferred the needles into Nessa's fingers, showing her how to hold them just so. "Somethin' I've learned from my Charlie goin' off to war is this: Sorrow looks back, worry looks around, but faith looks up. When we look to God for guidance and comfort, He helps us reach tomorrow. I know you're sad about the preacher, Nessa, and you might be sad for a long time, but you won't feel this way forever. Does that make any sense to you?"

"I think so." At the moment, Nessa wasn't sure if anything made sense anymore. She wanted to ask about the Applewoods and the two little graves she had seen in the cemetery.

But just then Fanny Jo stepped into the doorway, her baby on her shoulder. "Pardon me for interrupting," she said, "but I've received the most wonderful news from town."

"What is it, my dear?"

"My husband is on his way to Fort Larned for a five-day leave. He should be here tomorrow afternoon. The last time we saw each other was in Pennsylvania on our honeymoon. It's been so many months, I can hardly wait."

Mrs. Lockett moved her knitting basket to the top of her dresser. "Then we must get ready. Fanny Jo, you and your husband shall have this room — now don't argue with me — and the rest of us'll mind Kit. Come now, we've work to do." Turning to Nessa she said, "Honey, we'll finish our talk later."

After Nessa helped dry the supper dishes and put them away, she went upstairs to sit by her window at the head of her bed. Green jumped up, settling on the pillow, her moist nose touching Nessa's arm. The prairie had golden shadows from the setting sun. She could see soldiers on the Santa Fe Trail returning to the fort, their horses' manes swept back in the wind. Nessa was happy for Fanny Jo, that at long last her lieutenant would arrive and be able to hold their new baby.

While she watched the horizon, a star rose in the velvet blue sky. Within minutes, more stars appeared, like tiny lights from a distant town. Nessa opened the window to feel the cold air on her face.

In a few weeks she would turn fifteen. It was hard to believe that nearly a year had passed since her birthday. That day had brought the most terrible news: President Abraham Lincoln had been murdered by an assassin's bullet. His death had somehow given Nessa courage to flee the orphanage and begin a new life, the hardest decision she'd ever made.

Now as she looked out at the darkening prairie, she thought about the letter she needed to write and about yet another difficult decision.

Her brothers, cousins, and grandparents were in Wisconsin. They wanted her, and she desperately wanted them, too. But if she left Prairie River, she must also leave the family and friends she'd grown to love. Her students would be without a teacher, and she would miss meeting Captain Lockett when he returned home, as well as the orphaned drummer boy.

Another matter troubling her was that she hoped Albert would soon board a stagecoach headed this way, if he hadn't already. How could he and Nessa part once again?

She remembered her mother's prayer in the back of the cookbook. *Whatever is true . . . whatever is lovely . . . if there be any praise, think on these things.* Nessa admitted she could think all day about the good things in her life. She knew God loved her, but that still didn't change her dilemma.

Lord Jesus, please show me what to do. Except for Mary Ellen, I don't want to say good-bye to anyone! And maybe the Applewoods aren't so mean after all.

As she prayed, a thought occurred to her. What if, from her earnings, she could send for the twins? Surely her mother would have understood. She would have wanted all of her children to be together.

Nessa stroked Green's silky ears, practicing the words in her mind until they sounded just right. As her room grew dark, she lit a candle with the match Mrs. Lockett had given her after supper, then opened her trunk. The box of stationery was there with her pen.

Using the top of the chest for a table, Nessa arranged the paper, then dipped her quill in the jug of ink.

Dear Aunt Britta, she began.

About the Author

Kristiana Gregory was born in Los Angeles, California. She has always wanted to be a writer and received her first rejection letter (for a poem) at age eleven. After graduating from high school, she began taking a variety of college courses and jobs, including positions as a daily news reporter for the *San Luis Obispo Telegram-Tribune*, and a book reviewer for the *Los Angeles Times*, that helped prepare her for her writing career. Her first book, *Jenny of the Tetons*, won the Golden Kite Award for fiction. She has contributed numerous titles to Scholastic's Dear America and Royal Diaries series. Kristiana has also written several books about the Old West and California history. *Earthquake at Dawn*, her book about the 1906 San Francisco earthquake, won the 1993 California Book Award for best juvenile fiction.

Married for twenty-one years, she lives in Boise, Idaho, with her husband and two golden retrievers. Their two sons, college students, live nearby and often drop by around dinnertime.

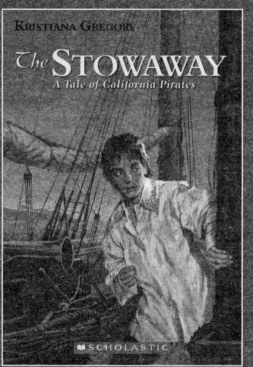

CJ'S ELECTION 2004

VISIT

www.scholastic.com/cj

Nominate Your Favorite Scholastic Girl Series and **ENTER FOR A CHANCE TO WIN** your very own NOMINATION BRACELET.

Visit www.nomination.us to see more charms and bracelets.

SCHOLASTIC

CJC